D0943980

Treasure Hunters

Keyword Cypher

E. A. House

EPIC Escape

An Imprint of EPIC Press
abdopublishing.com

Keyword Cypher
Treasure Hunters: Book #1

Written by E. A. House

Published by EPIC Press™
PO Box 398166
Minneapolis, MN 55439

Printed in the United States of America.

Cover design by Laura Mitchell
Images for cover art obtained from iStock and Shutterstock
Edited by Ryan Hume

Library of Congress Cataloging-in-Publication Data
Names: House, E.A., author.
Title: Keyword cypher/ by E.A. House
Description: Minneapolis, MN : EPIC Press, 2018 | Series: Treasure hunters; #1
Summary: Chris Kingsolver is heartbroken when his aunt Elsie dies in a car accident—and shocked to get a coded letter in the mail after her death. Elsie left Chris clues to the location of a lost treasure ship as an inheritance—if he, his cousin Carrie, and their new friend Maddison can find it.
Identifiers: LCCN 2017949807 | ISBN 9781680768763 (lib. bdg.) | ISBN 9781680768909 (ebook)
Subjects: LCSH: Adventure stories—Fiction. | Code and cipher stories—Fiction. | Family secrets—Fiction. | Treasure troves—Fiction | Young adult fiction.
Classification: DDC [FIC]—dc23
LC record available at http://lccn.loc.gov/2017949807

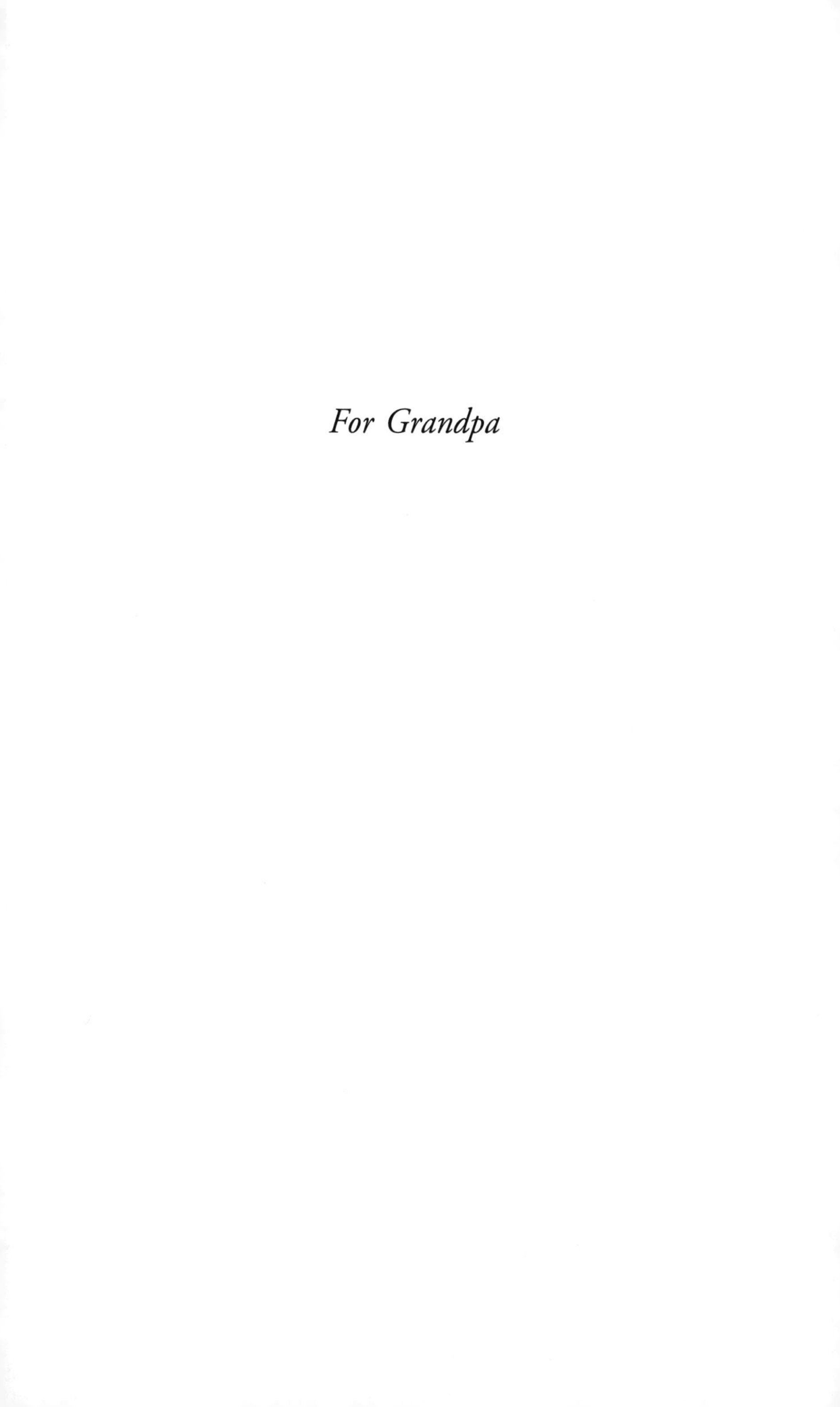

For Grandpa

CHAPTER ONE

AUNT ELSIE HAD LOVED LEAVING CLUES. WHEN Chris and his cousin Carrie had been small children in need of babysitting, Elsie had done puzzles with them, tried to teach them Morse code, and taught them how to make up secret codes so they could send each other messages that their parents and teachers couldn't read. Chris had loved this; Carrie had claimed it was an indication of his degenerate nature and then snatched her diary away from him before he could read it. Their aunt had almost always hidden an extra twenty-dollar bill in every Christmas and birthday gift, and on the rare occasions her niece and nephew complained about the way she was always hiding gift cards inside tricky puzzle boxes, she'd argue that figuring it out yourself was much more fun than just getting the present. Then she'd give them a bunch of clues, because Aunt Elsie wasn't actually sadistic and she did know that not everybody liked puzzles.

She died in May of 2016, in a hit-and-run that tossed her car into a ditch where it ruptured a fuel line and caught on fire. She was less than a mile from her house. The impact, the coroner said kindly at the inquest that ruled the crash accidental, broke her neck before the explosion, so she wouldn't have felt a thing. Not like that made anyone feel better. It wasn't much of a stretch to say that the loss of Elsie Kingsolver devastated the community of Archer's Grove, a small and mostly touristy island. Elsie Kingsolver had been the archivist at the Edgewater Maritime Archive since her return to the island fifteen years ago, right after the birth of her niece and nephew. She'd been from the area, too. The Kingsolvers went back several generations and had multiple sailors in their family tree.

Elsie had been the odd one out. Well-behaved shipping and merchant activity was in the family blood, enlivened by youngest sons who ran off to sea to become pirates, although the last documented case had been in the late 1920s. And Great-Uncle Robert had technically disappeared while smuggling moonshine in Kentucky. But the wandering gene usually struck the youngest child of the family, which should have been Robby, Carrie's father and Chris's uncle. Instead, he had earned a business degree, married an accountant named Helen, and gone into banking. His older brother Brian was a pharmacist. It had been Elsie, the eldest child and only girl, who went slightly off-kilter, devoting her life to history and old paper. And it was in this that she had excelled. A born teacher and a natural parent despite having no children of her own, she gave presentations on the archival collection of shipping charters that actually drew crowds, volunteered at the local historical society, and did programs with the local schools where she dressed up as a pirate and led a treasure hunt. Her funeral was packed with mourners.

Chris and Carrie read a poem about "slipping the surely bounds of earth" together, Carrie crying quietly and Chris staring fixedly out into the crowd, counting somber black-clad neighbors to keep himself from breaking down. It didn't help much. Carrie later suggested that picturing everyone in his or her underwear might have been a better idea but Chris thought that that would have been disrespectful. And he also came away confused by the number of people at the funeral that he didn't recognize. The funeral was held on an unfairly pleasant day, with a cloudless blue sky beaming down on the casket and a gentle breeze rustling the funeral flowers. All sorts of people had known and loved Aunt Elsie, so extended family, colleagues from grad school, and even the entire history department from the local college had come to pay their respects. So it was silly for Chris to expect to know everyone at the funeral. But a scattering of people in attendance were, quite frankly, sketchy looking.

There was a broad-shouldered man wearing sunglasses and lurking in the back of the crowd, wearing gloves on a warm, sunny day. There was a dark-haired family clustered under a willow tree, also all wearing sunglasses, the daughter squashed between her parents. She was clearly the same age as Chris, but not someone he'd ever seen at school. And when Chris walked back to the gravesite to fetch an aunt's purse, he found a tall man with the hood of his sweatshirt pulled up over a baseball cap standing in front of the very new grave. His silhouette was just the tiniest bit familiar. Chris actually called out to him, but the man tucked a bouquet of lilies into the already overflowing offerings of flowers and walked away without responding, head down and hands in his pockets. His eyes were shaded by a pair of aviator sunglasses. In fact, Chris decided, there were an awful lot of people wearing sunglasses at Elsie's funeral.

"Maybe because it's a sunny day?" Carrie suggested when Chris pointed this out to her at the wake. She was normally pretty pale, a side effect of having inherited the redhead gene from the Kingsolver side of the family, but today she was translucent and there were tear tracks on her cheeks. She had not, however, turned red with crying the way her brown-haired but very freckly cousin had. It was widely agreed that Elsie was—Elsie *had been*—particularly fond of Chris, who shared her interests and her free spirit, but Chris knew probably better than anyone else that Carrie had also had a special bond with their aunt. Aunt Elsie had delighted in Carrie's quick mind and undeniable skill at logic and puzzles, if despairing at her niece's stubborn refusal to be whimsical or suspend her disbelief for the fun of it.

"There are an awful lot of people wearing sunglasses *and* acting sketchy at this funeral," Chris said to clarify, and wasn't surprised when Carrie raised a skeptical eyebrow at him.

"Grief makes people do weird things, Chris," she pointed out. Since she normally didn't like chocolate but was currently eating her way through an entire platter of brownies, Chris couldn't possibly dispute this, but he did think Carrie was missing the point, which was that—

"Don't you dare tell me that the men in black are responsible for Aunt Elsie's death," Carrie said suddenly, her voice hitching on their aunt's name, and Chris swallowed his words, which had been to the effect that *someone* was behind Aunt Elsie's death. Possibly the Unabomber. "It's bad enough that—" She put her brownie down and swallowed.

"She shouldn't have died," Chris said miserably. "And she shouldn't have been killed by some jerk who didn't stop, and we should have been able to figure out who did it."

Which was what hurt the worst. True, someone was responsible for the car crash, but in the sense of having made a terrible mistake and then fleeing like a coward, which left the Kingsolver family with no closure. Not a fitting end to the life of a woman who had reasons for everything, even—one usually discovered later—her sudden whims. For example, Aunt Elsie had once suddenly decided to take her niece and nephew to Mexico over spring break. This had necessitated much rushing around in order to get Chris a passport, and the trip was widely regarded as final proof that Elsie had completely lost her marbles. But when Chris's dad surprised his wife with a trip to her beloved Ireland later that summer, he was able to keep it a secret up to the moment they got to the airport because the whole family, including Chris, had up-to-date passports. Aunt Elsie was proven both right and psychic.

That someone who loved leaving clues wherever she went had left no clues as to how she died made it so very hard to lay her to rest. It hurt, but even worse, it was out of character. Chris didn't think he was the only person who had somehow expected Aunt Elsie to either live forever or die in a way that was exceptionally well planned.

The letter arrived in the mail three days after the funeral.

Chris was supposed to sort the family mail when it came in but he did so irregularly, which had occasionally resulted in overdue bills. Once he had even racked up a library fine of fifty dollars and seventy-five cents by not noticing the mailed overdue notice. It had been a book on money management, an irony that Carrie had never quite forgiven him for and intended never to let him forget. Chris really spent more time in trouble for forgetting to sort the mail than he did actually sorting it. But in the wake of the funeral his parents had been less inclined to scold and more inclined to let things slide, and so it was five days after the funeral, when he couldn't deal with wondering why Aunt Elsie had died or who the people in sunglasses were at the funeral or what the girl he didn't recognize was doing there, that Chris decided he had to do something and so actually did his chores.

School was not a distraction. School had ended the day after the funeral on a vaguely menacing note for Chris and Carrie, both sixteen-year-old rising juniors: the summer reading assignment had been three pages long, and had been dispensed with strict instruction to "skimp reading at your own peril." Then there had been a class assembly in which the soon-to-be juniors were informed by the guidance counselor that they needed to start seriously thinking about their future plans, especially college admissions. This was good advice, and advice that Carrie had taken with something approaching panic, judging by how many admission applications she had already filled out. But Chris already had enough to worry about. And Mrs. Melliflure, the guidance counselor for the junior and senior classes, had spent so many of the past months dealing with panicked, last-minute college admissions that she had developed her end-of-year twitch, scaring students away rather than encouraging them to fill out applications. Not yet ready to face the stress of college admissions and not yet ready to go out and get a summer job, Chris had nothing to do at all but think, yet wanted more than anything to avoid doing so. Thus the mail sorting.

"Bill," Chris muttered to himself, sifting through a large and slightly damp stack of mail, "bill, bill—should have cleaned the mailbox out after that storm two weeks ago—*National Geographic*, letter from Grandma, letter from Aunt Elsie—"

Chris stopped, turned the letter over, and stared

at it. Aunt Elsie had not been one of those people who refused to deal with computers, but she'd been very fond of sending letters to her friends and family, usually full of fun facts, amusing anecdotes, and clipped-out cartoons. The letter now trembling between his fingers looked no different from any of the other letters Aunt Elsie had sent him, right down to the return address, and had been tucked into the newspaper dated the day before the funeral. It was, in short, a letter from beyond the grave.

Or, as Chris realized when he peeled the envelope open in the privacy of his bedroom and actually read the letter, a perfectly ordinary letter from Aunt Elsie. In swooping blue cursive—her youngest brother hated blue-inked pens with a passion, and Aunt Elsie had used exclusively blue ballpoint since the eighth grade in joking retaliation for That One Time Brian Stole My Chocolate Bar—she talked about her plans for the summer library program, asked if Chris would be interested in dressing up as Captain Hook, and described the mathematical formula for determining the probability of intelligent life in the universe. She'd drawn an apologetic mosquito in the corner of the letter, looking guilty for biting people, and had taped a cartoon of an elephant tap-dancing to the back. And then at the very end she'd added a non sequitur:

p.s. when you do the Christmas cards start with me.

"Aunt Elsie, what are you trying to tell me?" Chris asked the letter. Being a piece of paper it didn't say anything. Then the door to his bedroom flew open and he yelped and threw the letter under the bed. He needn't have, it was only his mom.

"Chris, honey," she said, holding up the dampest of the bills by one corner, "did you start sorting the mail and then get distracted?"

"I—yeah," Chris said. "Sorry, Mom."

"Well, I'd like you to finish it at some point," his mom said. "And then go find a clean dress shirt, one of the letters in the pile was from your aunt's lawyer. We need to go start settling her estate tomorrow."

The instant she left, Chris scrambled under the bed and fished out the letter, along with a surprising number of socks plus one of his dress shirts—very crumpled—and settled down to think. Chris never did the Christmas cards. One year he had taken two ordinary store-bought Christmas cards, cut the embossed cover off one, glued it to the cover of the other with his gift to Carrie sealed inside, and then apologetically told Carrie he hadn't been able to find her anything but the card. His parents had been irritated, Aunt Elsie had been amused and delighted, and Carrie had found the gift cards hidden inside unfairly quickly, considering how little she approved of gag gifts. But the Great Gift Card Debacle, as it was commonly referred to, made Chris the last person anyone let near the Christmas cards. If Aunt Elsie pretended to assume he was in charge of writing them, then she clearly meant him to see it as a clue. But a clue to what?

Chris was still puzzling over the letter the next day, while avoiding his mother's wrath—he hadn't *tried* to outgrow his best shirt and tie—and wondering how long it would be before she tried to make him apply for a summer job again. The afternoon was spent in the conference room of Aunt Elsie's lawyer's office, with the Kingsolver family squeezed around a table, fidgeting. But then, halfway through a tedious discussion of who was to sort out what part of the money Aunt Elsie had left to everyone, Chris realized that Aunt Elsie's lawyer might have known about the letter. Aunt Elsie's lawyer was Mr. Protheridge, who was a small bald man with impressively bat-like ears. He wore a tweed vest and a watch chain with such determination that he made the outfit work, and when Chris pounced on him as his parents and aunt and uncle started discussing the terms of the will, Protheridge blinked and nodded.

"Ah, yes, the letter," he said, shuffling papers. "Elsie had that arranged well in advance."

Across the room, Carrie looked up sharply from where she was studying the locket Aunt Elsie had left her, and then refused to meet Chris's eyes.

"So, when did she actually write it?" Chris asked.

"Well, presumably sometime the week before she passed," Mr. Protheridge said, and when he spotted

Chris's confused look, he continued, "Elsie asked me to mail a letter to the address she specified in the event of her death when she first wrote up her will several years ago. But to be honest I thought it was a provision she'd forgotten about. She didn't give me a letter to mail until the week before last."

"Did she say *why*?" Chris asked.

"Not to me," Mr. Protheridge said kindly. "She just dropped by quite late one night, reminded me about the provision she'd made for mailing a letter in the event of her death, and handed over a letter. It was addressed to you. I assume you received it?"

Chris, suddenly aware of being in a public space with any number of ears about, mumbled something noncommittal and fled from the kindly and now confused lawyer, to sit in the car until the rest of his family wandered out of the office.

"Aunt Elsie was trying to tell us something before she

died," Chris said to Carrie later that evening. They were sitting on opposite ends of the sofa in Carrie's living room, not really watching a home-improvement show and listening to the faint sound of their parents talking together outside in the backyard.

Carrie mumbled noncommittally and flipped the page of her magazine. She was turning the locket—it was brass, engraved to look like a compass and with a picture of a ship in full sail on the inside—over and over on its chain. It had been the one material thing Aunt Elsie left to Carrie.

"You don't think there's something really wrong with how she died?" Chris asked. "And then she left me that letter right before her death? And when has Aunt Elsie ever done something that wasn't secretly a puzzle?" Carrie shot him an evil look and deliberately turned up the volume on the television. They sat together in silence, the tension thicker than the humidity they were inside trying to escape.

"Carrie!" Chris finally snapped when he couldn't take it anymore. She looked up from her magazine with a wild-eyed expression that would have been a warning if Chris hadn't been so angry. "What's the *matter* with you? Do you even care?"

Carrie was widely and justly considered the calmest and most sensible Kingsolver child, so the fact that she hurled the magazine to the floor with enough violence to rattle the coffee table and then went directly to screamingly angry was a shock to Chris. "Of course I care!" she howled, "but unlike *you* Aunt Elsie didn't leave me a stupid letter! Everyone's all 'oh, Carrie's the sweet, sensible one, we'll let her do all the memorial stuff while we let stupid slacker Chris mourn in peace because he was'"—she made violent air quotes—"'"*so close* to his aunt. It's not like Elsie even liked *Carrie*.'" She was now crying. "And it's not like I can think there's something wrong with the police report either because that's Chris's area of insanity and I've got to be totally fine! I'm the *mature* one! So take your letter and go—go *choke on it*!"

And before Chris could say anything at all, she had

fled the living room and slammed the door of her bedroom so hard paint chips fell off the doorframe.

She did not come out of her room for the rest of the night, even when her mom poked her head in and asked if she wanted any caramel ice cream, and Carrie loved caramel ice cream as much as she generally hated chocolate. Chris was forced to sit at the kitchen table, and eat ice cream, and to talk politely about his summer plans to his aunts and uncles all by himself. It was exhausting, and stressful, and Carrie's outburst had hit a couple of sore spots—Chris knew he wasn't as responsible as Carrie was, but he wasn't a complete slacker—and all in all he was very relieved when his parents decided it was time to walk the three houses down the street to their own house.

"You were a good sport today," his dad said as they were collecting shoes in the living room in preparation for leaving. "I know it must have been hard."

Chris shrugged. His anger had faded, and guilt was now creeping in to replace it, squeezing into the spaces not yet filled with grief. "I didn't mean to fight with Carrie," he said.

"I know, kiddo," his dad said gently. "Carrie didn't mean to fight with you either—she's having as much trouble as you are with this but you let yourself be upset and she hasn't yet."

"I didn't mean to—" Chris started, and then jumped a mile when Carrie yelled,

"You never *mean* to do anything!" from her bedroom. He'd forgotten it was just down the hall from the living room.

"I still think there's something up with the letter," Chris said to the shut door in question, his stubborn conviction that there was a mystery here warring with guilt for dragging Carrie into something she didn't want to do while she was grieving, and with the knowledge that he should really leave Carrie alone until she cooled off.

"Well then," Carrie snarled, "why don't you just *figure it out*?"

Chapter Two

And so Chris tried. He got up the next morning and sat down at his desk with the letter and decided, then and there, that he would find the hidden message if it killed him. He looked at the letter in sunlight and bathed it in lemon juice to see if either method revealed something written in invisible ink. He tried every letter substitution he knew and a few he made up on the spot, and finally he gave up, threw the letter into the trash can, and said, more or less to himself and the desk lamp, "This is *impossible.*"

"Nah, just wildly improbable," Carrie said, directly

and unexpectedly behind him, and Chris gave an undignified yelp and jumped a foot in the air.

"Where did you come from?" he asked.

Carrie sighed. "I came in through the front door," she said patiently, rummaging the letter out of the trash, "like a sane person? I'm here to help with the letter."

"I'm pretty sure I read too much into it," Chris mumbled, feeling uncomfortably guilty. It was one thing to decide that Aunt Elsie had left him a coded message in her last letter and waste all *his* time looking for it, but dragging Carrie into a quest that was likely a coping method wasn't fair to her. She was probably—Chris could even admit to himself—having a harder time of it, since there hadn't even been a goodbye letter for her and he'd kind of held that over her head and now he was *still* making a fuss over Aunt Elsie paying special attention to him even after her death and—

"Did you check for invisible ink?" Carrie asked suddenly. Apparently sometime between slamming the door in his face last night and turning up in his house this morning she'd decided their fight didn't matter.

"Yeah, got zip," Chris said. "And she always sent us invisible ink letters on blue paper anyway."

"I know," Carrie said, with something in her voice that made Chris sit up and realize she was holding the envelope, not the letter. "And did you notice what color the envelope was?"

The envelope was blue. A familiar, pretty awful shade of blue that Chris and Carrie had both loved as children and subsequently grown out of, but more importantly the exact shade of blue that Aunt Elsie had regularly used for invisible ink letters. Chris scrambled up the sponge and some lemon juice and swiped a corner, and joined Carrie in a delighted "Yes!" when a thin line of Aunt Elsie's neat capital letters appeared. Then they both drooped again.

"And it's also in a code," Carrie said as they looked at the envelope.

"Now do you agree that this is impossible?" Chris

asked, re-reading the letter for the fortieth time, and was surprised when Carrie shook her head.

"No. I can't believe I'm saying this, but your wrongful death theory is actually starting to make sense if Aunt Elsie went to this much trouble to hide a message in a letter to the family slacker."

"Start with me," Chris said to himself, actually managing to ignore Carrie's traditional jab. "She left me one obvious clue, and that was 'p.s. when you do the Christmas cards, start with me,' so what does she—hey, wait!"

"Not actually going anywhere," Carrie said, picking up the pad of scratch paper covered in previous attempts to work out substitutions and frowning thoughtfully at it. Chris, who had just had a revelation, made desperate grabby hands at it.

"Do you remember how Aunt Elsie started teaching us codes when we were six?"

"Start by reversing the alphabet, and then—oh!" Carrie said. Aunt Elsie had taught them fun with codes by showing them the reverse alphabet one, and then how you could substitute any letter for any other letter as long as you kept it consistent or had a key.

The first thing they'd ever done was use C for A, since both their names started with a C. And if you started with ELSI and left off the second E, so you didn't repeat letters for ABCD . . . "'Dear Chris,'" Chris read, "'smart boy, if you are reading this then I am dead.'"

Chris stopped and looked up at Carrie. She was wide eyed, and without Chris asking, she quietly went over and closed his bedroom door.

"'So you and Carrie need to do me a favor,'" Chris continued, reading from the page. "'In my office at work there is a floorboard with a burn mark. I hid a box under that floorboard, and I need you two to find that box and look at what I put inside. Remember that I love both of you. Start with me.'"

"Okay," Carrie said. "I—actually I kind of suspected something like this?"

"You suspected Aunt Elsie of . . . of secret Indiana Jones adventures?" Chris asked. Honestly he'd *often* suspected Aunt Elsie of having secret Indiana Jones-style adventures, but he'd always had enough self-respect not to tell Carrie.

"No," Carrie said, "but out of everyone we know, who is—*was* most likely to discover a secret someone might kill for?"

"Aunt Elsie," Chris admitted. "Do you think we should tell our parents?"

Carrie hissed. "Ehhh . . . no?"

"Carrie!"

"I'm not sure they'd believe us," Carrie admitted. "I'm not sure *I* believe us, but I'm really suspicious and my grief is making me do risky things."

"Okay . . . " Chris said. "Then what *do* you think we should do?"

Carrie looked at her watch and groaned. "Well, I'm about to be late. I promised Mrs. Hadler I'd help sort files in the school office today, so—talk about it more tonight?"

"You could skip?" Chris suggested, and then quailed under the death glare Carrie gave him in response.

Mrs. Hadler was the school secretary and Carrie had been her office aide during a study hall. Mrs. Hadler was also the most terrifying secretary Chris had ever laid eyes on, so turning up tardy when you'd promised to help her out was out of the question, even if she did by some fluke of nature actually like you.

Mrs. Hadler actually liked Carrie. In fact, she liked Carrie enough that when the school district told Mrs. Hadler to digitize the school's student records before the start of the next school year, Mrs. Hadler offered Carrie a summer job sorting student files and then entering the data. Aunt Elsie had raised an eyebrow at this part-time summer job because of the gigantic confidentiality issues it raised, and then sighed and told Carrie to be very careful not to do anything that could be considered an invasion of privacy, nor to believe everything she found in the files. The incident her junior year involving the VW Bug and the high school chess team, Aunt Elsie had added, was a fluke in her otherwise flawless record, no matter what Carrie's father or the guidance counselor's files said. Chris's mom had made several pointed comments about how at least Carrie *had* a summer job, and Chris was still holding out a faint hope she'd drop the subject of *him* getting one.

"Okay!" Chris said as Carrie scrambled her scattered purse together. "Go help Mrs. Hadler, and I'll do something productive while waiting."

"Yeah," Carrie said distractedly, slinging her bag over her shoulder, but then she stopped halfway out the door, turned fully around to face Chris, and actually pointed a finger at him. "But don't do anything stupid," she said.

Since in Chris's experience Carrie usually preferred to let him do something stupid and then look horrified at the result, she was clearly worried. So in an effort to show that he was taking the whole situation seriously, Chris went out of his way to do things around the house that weren't stupid. He started by finishing up the mail sorting and then cleaned his room, in the process finding an incredible number of ballpoint pens that did not work, fifteen dollars in spare change, and far too many hair bands considering he didn't have long hair. These he collected in a cup on his desk in case Carrie wanted them back. Then he went to answer the ringing house phone, which turned out to be the library, calling about the overdue books, and flicked the hairbands all over the living room while reassuring the librarian that he would find that copy of *The Kon-Tiki Expedition.* Somewhere. Then he did a load of laundry, lost his patience, and was in the process of heading out the door to start tearing up floorboards at the Edgewater Archive when it occurred to him that this was exactly what Carrie was afraid he'd do.

"Okay," Chris said to himself, "something not stupid." Well, Carrie could hardly object to his looking up the hours of operation for the Archive, along with any available floor plans and maybe some Google Maps images of the back door, because Chris and Carrie were too used to visiting the Archive whenever they wanted and being let in by their aunt, who'd had a key. And it was possible—and possibly probable—that in this case they might need to break into the Archive under the cover of darkness to pull up the floorboards.

The small part of Chris's mind known as his common sense pointed out, in a voice that sounded a lot like Carrie's, that they might do better to just walk in the door and say they wanted to clear out Aunt Elsie's office for their parents. Chris sighed to himself, consigned the visions of cat burglary to his overactive imagination, and pulled up the Edgewater Maritime Archive's webpage.

X X X

As its name was intended to suggest, the Edgewater Maritime Archive was a small institution devoted to preserving the documentation of Florida's seafaring past. And according to the Archive's mission statement proudly displayed over an artfully taken picture of the front doors:

THE EDGEWATER ARCHIVE FOCUSES ON

COLLECTING BOOKS, PAPERS, CHARTS, AND MAPS THAT ARE ABOUT OR BY THE EARLY EXPLORERS AND SETTLERS OF FLORIDA'S COASTS, AND IS ESPECIALLY PROUD OF ITS COLLECTION OF SPANISH MISSION CHURCH DOCUMENTS AND SMALL BUT WELL-SELECTED COLLECTION OF SHIP-WRECK ARTIFACTS AND RELATED DOCUMENTS.

Chris had read that blurb off the website, his aunt's paperwork, and even the Archive's front doors so often he had it memorized, but seeing the familiar words and knowing that the institution had lost his aunt hurt. In fact, a lot of the research Chris set out to do about the Archive was unexpectedly painful.

The first and most painful thing was the scrolling banner, which was still displaying Aunt Elsie's "Lost Ships of the 1717 Fleet" web exhibit. It was intended to be the first part of a much larger exhibit on Florida's lost and buried treasure, and Aunt Elsie had been in her element searching out gold and silver coins, fragments of ships' hulls, letters and journals from long-ago mariners, and paintings of various shipwrecks.

The 1717 Fleet had been her jumping-off point for the exhibit, because persistent rumors suggested that Archer's Grove might have been the end of the line for one of the still-lost and thus still-full-of-gold treasure ships of the fleet. Aunt Elsie had been swamped with research for the past four months, and the very last time Chris had spent the night at his aunt's house he'd spent the morning getting an impromptu history lesson about Spanish treasure ships.

This was because Chris's parents had been square dancing competitively since college. They'd *met* at a dance, which made significantly more sense to people when Chris explained that his father had gone to school in Iowa on an excellent scholarship. But this meant, in turn, that the Kingsolvers were sometimes out of town on the weekends for square-dancing competitions, and although they really had no problem with Chris staying home alone, he generally just spent the night at his aunt's. In fact, Chris's dad was of the opinion that Chris was safer home alone than in his sister's obviously haunted house. This was probably why Aunt Elsie had left her house to him, to be kept for Chris when he turned twenty-one. Aunt Elsie had a suspect sense of humor.

But leaving aside the question of whether the old Georgian mansion was haunted, the history of the 1717 Fleet had been explained to Chris when he wandered downstairs that Saturday morning a few months ago and found Aunt Elsie eating carrot muffins and taking notes from three books at once.

"So," she'd said when he hit the last step, which moaned at the slightest pressure and was probably where the ghost stories came from, "want to hear about another lost opportunity for a Hollywood blockbuster?"

Chris had agreed, and Aunt Elsie had flicked a few pages and begun.

"In the year 1717, following several years of blocked shipping between the Americas and Europe, a fleet of Spanish galleons congregated in Cuba for the trip to Spain. They numbered either twelve or thirteen, depending on the account, and were loaded with precious metals, mainly silver and gold in coin form—honest-to-goodness pieces of eight and something called cobs—along with silverware and Chinese porcelain, and the massive dowry of the Princess Annamarie, all of *that* loaded aboard the still-lost *San Telmo*. They say," she added, "that the princess's dowry was six times that of any previous dowry, and that it included not only several famously fine-wrought golden crowns but also an emerald the size and shape of a goose egg and a dagger studded with diamonds. Anyway, the fleet was en route to Spain in July of 1717 when, having been delayed into hurricane season by the necessity of waiting for merchants to stuff the ships with treasure and for the last pieces of the princess's dowry to turn up—" Aunt Elsie made an 'as you do' gesture with both her hands "—it encountered a hurricane and sank near the Florida coast. Recovery of the *vast* amount of gold and silver the ships were carrying began immediately, but salvage, treasure hunting, pirates, and uncertainty over just where some of the ships sank hindered the search, and today there are still ships left unaccounted for and coins from the wreck washing up on Florida beaches."

Aunt Elsie had shuffled her papers importantly, and grinned at Chris. It was her "take *that*, Indiana Jones" grin, and usually indicated that she was about to make life very interesting for everyone around her.

"The plan," Aunt Elsie had added, "is for a web exhibit showcasing the letters we have from some Spanish sailors after the fact, and then, if I can cajole certain museums, for a bigger in-house exhibit using some artifacts, and maybe an extra exhibit on the long lost *San Telmo.*"

"Sooo, do we have a new summer project?" Chris had asked. He'd been poking through Aunt Elsie's selection of muffins at the time, and so hadn't been looking at her face. But if he remembered correctly, there had been just the tiniest hesitation, just enough to make Chris look up to see if Aunt Elsie had heard him, before she'd hummed and shaken her head.

"You would need a very good, very new lead to go looking for the *San Telmo*," she'd said, cutting a muffin in half. "Or some advancements in search technology. Neither of which I see happening, so we're just gonna have to spend the summer keeping Carrie from getting at our sealed student records."

"Shoot," Chris had said, and there the matter had rested. He hadn't known, then, that the web exhibit would be the very last exhibit Aunt Elsie did for the museum.

She had already put together a map, several short videos, a narrative of the history of the 1717 Fleet, a picture gallery that advertised the Archive's collection of first-hand accounts of the aftermath of the wreck and its excellent, if tiny, collection of gold and silver coins, and had been in the final stages of preparation for the physical exhibit when she'd died. Someone had added a discreet memorial link to Aunt Elsie's staff page below the watercolor of "An artist's rendition of the *San Telmo* mid-catastrophe." After sparing a moment to wonder, as he always did, if the *San Telmo* really had a prow carved to look like an octopus, Chris followed the link. He grinned at the picture in which Aunt Elsie was wearing her famous historically inaccurate pirate hat and was about to go back to looking for a plan of the building when something on the staff page caught his eye.

The 'House Archivist' position was already filled. She'd been gone for two weeks, and already the board had hired somebody to fill her position? Really? They'd hired a somebody named Kevin McRae, in fact—no picture yet—just a two-sentence blurb about how he was "looking forward to preserving and sharing the treasures of our Florida history." Feeling both justifiably angry and a little unnerved—because surely you didn't usually fill an archivist position this fast—Chris re-read the tiny blurb, checked the staff directory to see if they had a picture somewhere else, and finally, when that yielded nothing, turned to Google. When Carrie came by at around five in the evening he was trying and failing to find Kevin McRae on Facebook and LinkedIn, and so involved was he in his futile search that Carrie managed to sneak up on him again.

"I wasn't trying to sneak up on you!" Carrie said irritably while Chris had a minor spaz attack from the unexpected sensation of a hot hand on his shoulder. "And I've been outside in the humidity, what did you expect?" She sat down with a huff on the exercise ball that Chris's mom had bought herself and then decided never to use. Chris liked to bounce it out the attic window when he was bored.

"I was researching," Chris said.

"I'll admit I'm impressed. And worried—did you move from that spot at all today?"

Chris admitted that he *maybe* had, if one counted bathroom breaks and putting a lunch together. "But I was going to find a floor plan of the Archive before I realized you'd just insist we walk in the front door, and then I had to look up this Kevin McRae guy."

"Kevin McRae?" Carrie asked.

"The archivist they've *already* hired to replace Aunt

Elsie," Chris said. "Don't tell me I'm just being paranoid. This is getting really weird."

Carrie was quiet for a moment, wobbling back and forth a bit on the exercise ball. "I wasn't going to," she said.

"Good," Chris said. "Because I'm seriously starting to think we need to go to the police about this—"

"Actually," Carrie interrupted, bouncing suddenly off the exercise ball and to her feet as though she'd made an unpleasant but necessary decision, "I was going to ask you to come look at something for me? We've got an hour before anybody expects us for dinner."

Chapter Three

They actually had more like forty-five minutes, not nearly enough time to do what Carrie wanted to do, which was retrace Aunt Elsie's last fatal drive. Aunt Elsie had lived in what she considered necessary peace and quiet and what Chris's dad considered a hellish pit, which when you averaged it out meant that she'd lived two miles outside of town in a large, crumbling Georgian manor house. It had once been painted a white that had since turned dingy gray, and it dripped with Spanish moss and had a distinctly haunted aura. The house wasn't remote but it was isolated, and the winding road where Aunt Elsie had died was barely two lanes wide. At the last curve before the house there was an off-kilter crossroads at the crest of a hill, and a car had run the stop sign coming out of a dip in the road and rammed Elsie's car into a ditch. There were still scorch marks in the grass, and although her car had been moved, caution tape was still wrapped around some of the trees at the site of the accident.

Carrie pulled her mom's car into the driveway of the now-empty house, parked, and then marched across the crossroads to just before the crest of the hill. It was a significant dip in the road that you really couldn't see out of, and it'd caused accidents before when someone went into the dip, missed the stop sign, and breezed into another car on the way out.

"It rained the day she died," Carrie said when Chris caught up to her. She was standing in the grass at the edge of the intersecting road, which was dirt and gravel. The main road Aunt Elsie had been on was blacktop. "I checked the weather report for the month—know how we've been in a dry-ish spell?"

"Yeah," Chris said, thinking of the soggy mail he

hadn't sorted fully and not sure where his cousin was going with this.

"It was dry the day before, and hasn't done more than sprinkle since," Carrie said. "Now I came out here after work, today. And look at this."

She pointed and, to make it clearer in the gradually darkening light, pulled a flashlight out of her purse and shined it on a pair of tire tracks pressed deeply into the road. They were worn but still clearly visible in the dried sandy mud.

"You think that's from the car that killed her?" Chris asked.

Carrie sighed, and actually looked around as though she thought somebody might be in the trees watching her. "I think it might be from the car that murdered her," she said quietly and in a rush. When Chris did nothing but stare at her, she twirled the flashlight nervously a few times and continued, "This whole dip in the road gets pretty muddy when it rains—as a matter of fact there's a spot back there where I think you could get really stuck really easily, but if you look at the tire tracks? These tire tracks? They're really clear here and nowhere else. I think somebody was sitting here, in their car, waiting."

"Okay," Chris said, because there *were* no clearer tire tracks than the ones she'd pointed out. "But that could mean a lot of things—"

"Also, somebody had to have been sitting here for a while," Carrie added, "because there's an oily spot in the road right between the tire tracks."

"Oh," Chris said.

"Yeah."

"You don't really think—" Chris started to say, because this was Carrie, who did the right and normal and sane thing and was just a little bit ashamed of the treasure hunts of their youth. Carrie, who found a reasonable and rational explanation for everything. Carrie, who was now gathering a whole bunch of innocent-looking facts into a pile that screamed "murder" to the heavens.

Somewhere in the dense forest a twig snapped and something crashed through the underbrush, startling them both and saving Chris from voicing his own suspicions aloud.

"Come on," Carrie said, suddenly turning off her flashlight and striding back to the car so quickly Chris had to jog to keep up with her.

"You think Aunt Elsie was murdered?" Chris asked as he climbed into the car, the need to move and a nagging feeling of urgency giving him the bravery to blurt it out.

"She never did anything without a reason, Chris," Carrie said, starting the car and locking the doors. "Never. Sometimes we didn't understand the reason—I still have no clue why she habitually reversed the first and last address when she was writing out directions for herself, remember when she got Dad lost in a Cyprus swamp? But . . . "

"At some point she would have explained why, yeah, I know," Chris agreed.

"So why would she leave you an 'if you're reading this I've been murdered' letter if she hadn't at least considered the possibility of being murdered? Aunt

Elsie liked you, she wouldn't play with your raging paranoia like that."

"I do not have a problem with paranoia," Chris said. "And I think that car is following us."

There *were* headlights glued to their back bumper. They'd been too caught up with each other to register when the car pulled in behind them and it was now too dark to see much, but there were headlights behind them. It could have been nothing and probably *was* nothing, but it made for a deeply uncomfortable drive home, and Chris may have been more defensive of his paranoid streak as a result. *It's more or less real,* he told himself. But it wasn't as bad as Carrie made it out to be. When the car following them peeled off one street from their house it was a huge relief, and the argument about paranoia lost half its heat, although it didn't stop completely. Chris and Carrie had a couple of set arguments that were mostly just a comfortable way of passing the time.

They were consequently still arguing the exact point at which everyone really was out to get you when they pulled into Chris's driveway and parked, so it took them a moment to register that there was one more car in the Kingsolver gravel drive than normal. Then the figure rummaging in the backseat of the Jeep straightened up and Carrie yelped.

"Professor Griffin!"

"Smaller Kingsolvers!" Professor Griffin exclaimed, smiling. He was his usual tall, tanned, commanding presence—he could have played a sea captain in an action movie. He was a professor of oceanography and so in fact *did* spend a lot of time out on the ocean being commanding—although his smile was dimmer than usual and there were worry lines around his face that hadn't been there when Chris and Carrie had last seen him.

They had seen him last a month ago, when he'd waved them off at the pier. Willis Griffin had been both a colleague and a friend of Elsie Kingsolver's since they'd met in Geology 101 at the University of Florida, although he'd gone on to teach oceanography at a college level and she'd gone into the library sciences. Aunt Elsie didn't talk much about her college days (except to remind Chris and Carrie that she expected them to attend), but when she did, Professor Griffin featured prominently. They had gone in very different directions after college but then had found each other over and over again in their professional lives. Professor Griffin sometimes joked that Elsie was afraid to let him out of her sight, for fear of him really finding a cursed treasure and being haunted by it for the rest of his life. For the past six years Professor Griffin had worked with Aunt Elsie at the satellite college campus where he taught geography and oceanography; they had long worked together on research projects, and he was a close friend of the family. He had been almost the only person not at the funeral.

"I only just got back," Professor Griffin said, giving Carrie a hug and Chris an arm around the shoulders.

"And I am so, so sorry about Elsie, and so very sorry I couldn't be back in time for the funeral."

"It's okay," Carrie said, poking her nose into the grocery bag Professor Griffin was holding and grinning at what she saw.

"Not really," Professor Griffin said. "I should have, oh I don't know, jumped over the side and swum home for the funeral. Blasted Atlantic Ocean, deep and vast."

"Well," Carrie said, "everybody did miss you at the funeral. But that wouldn't have worked and anyway you'd have had to pay your respects in a wetsuit."

"But we knew you were out in the middle of the Atlantic with no way to get back in time," Chris said. "So nobody blames you. Or at least I don't."

"I don't either," Carrie said, pulling a jar of maraschino cherries out of the bag.

"That is because you two are angels," Professor Griffin said, an arm around each of them as they walked up the drive toward to the house, "who I'm planning to ply with ice cream and pictures taken from

Moby after dinner so you'll forgive me my absence—drat and botheration!" The professor was buzzing. Or rather, ringing.

"Your . . . hat is ringing," Carrie pointed out.

"Ah," Professor Griffin said after patting down his pockets, shaking out his jacket, and finally taking off his hat and removing his phone from where it had been tucked in the inside band. "It's my phone! I'm afraid I need to answer this person. You two go on ahead," he said, shooing them into the house. He wandered back down the driveway. "Yes, this is he," Chris heard him say into the phone.

"Carrie!" Chris's mom exclaimed. "You brought groceries?"

"Professor Griffin did, Aunt Bree," Carrie explained. "He's outside answering a phone call right now."

"Ah," Professor Griffin said from the doorway, "so sorry about that, former student on the other end, he was in a bit of a quandary. Hopefully I've steered him in the right direction. What's for dinner, Bree?"

Dinner was livelier and happier than it had been recently. Chris and Carrie were used to eating dinner together since they lived down the street from each other, and it was almost normal to be having chicken and rice with both sets of parents and Professor Griffin. Talking about the professor's research into ocean floor fauna and the pictures brought up by *Moby*, Professor Griffin's very small and very accident-prone submersible, was almost entirely normal. Almost normal, that is, except for the absence of Aunt Elsie, which was like having a giant hole at the head of the table that everyone could sense. Luckily Professor Griffin had a gift for distraction.

"I brought ice cream in memory of Elsie," he said as he helped clear away the dinner plates. In almost any other family this would have been a simple comment on dessert. The Kingsolvers were not a normal family, so there was a wail of mingled horror and delight at the news.

"Willis, you didn't," Uncle Robby said.

"Oh *no*," Chris's mom added.

"Oh yes, I did," Professor Griffin said, his eyes a little teary and a lot amused. "Elsie would've *insisted* on fake cherry cordial chip at the wake. Do you want her to haunt us?"

"I hate maraschino cherries," Uncle Robby said, putting his head down on the table without even checking if his plate was still in the way. "And now I have gravy on my nose."

Aunt Elsie had had a cultured palette (whatever that meant, Chris had never been sure), a wide range of tastes, and a willingness to try anything once, including scorpion lollipops. But she had also had a horrifying weakness for cheap chocolate-chip ice cream with maraschino cherries poured over the top. She had served it at every holiday get-together, even Easter and Halloween, and it was a dessert that divided the Kingsolver family more thoroughly than even Aunt Helen and Chris's mom supporting different political parties. Half the family loved it, half the family hated it; Chris could not stand maraschino cherries and Aunt Helen was suddenly lactose intolerant whenever the dessert showed up. Professor Griffin—not a blood relative but still a member of the family—regarded chocolate chip ice cream and maraschino cherries as a nostalgic treat, enjoying some whenever it was available. He had brought two family-sized tubs of the super-cheap chocolate chip ice cream and an enormous jar of maraschino cherries with him.

"Your aunt came up with this idea," he told Chris, spooning cherries into a bowl. It was a comfortable habit rather than anything else, because Chris *knew* the story of the chocolate-chip-cherry-ice-cream-of-doom by heart. "We were freshmen in college and she wanted cherry-chocolate-chip ice cream, but had no car and little money and the convenience store across the street only had chocolate chip."

"She couldn't just be happy with chocolate chip?" Chris asked, like he almost always did.

"It's not that bad," Carrie mumbled around a mouthful of cherries.

"It's weird and pointless," Chris said. "We couldn't just have cherry cordial chip from the store instead?"

But he put cherries in his bowl anyway, because the point was not ice cream but Aunt Elsie.

"Most of the best things in life are weird and pointless," the professor said. "Want to see a very cranky shark that tried to chew *Moby*'s camera off?"

"Sure," Chris said. "But Professor Griffin—"

"Hmm?" The professor was sorting out pictures of a very irritable electric eel and a very sad-looking submersible and paying only partial attention to Chris, which was just perfect for his purposes.

"I was wondering . . . " Chris said, hoping that his nerves would look like grief (to some degree they were). " . . . if it would be okay for me to help pack up Aunt Elsie's office?"

"Oh!" Professor Griffin said. "Yes, of course! That is," he added, "if it's okay with your parents? It needs to be done soon so we have somewhere to put the new archivist and I'm sure Elsie would have wanted you to do it. Most of her personal papers were to go to you and Carrie, did you know that?"

"Yes," Carrie said under her breath, "but not why . . . "

"Then do you mind if I come over to Edgewater tomorrow and start packing stuff up?" Chris asked, ignoring Carrie's aside. He wasn't even sure it was aimed at him. They had all known, since the meeting with Aunt Elsie's lawyer, that almost all of Aunt Elsie's papers had been left to Chris and Carrie. Chris was honestly puzzled by this bequest because most of Aunt Elsie's papers were boring, especially the ones that detailed what to do if the Archive flooded. The sixty-page disaster-preparedness manual focused to an incredible degree on how to halt mold damage, which Chris just did not find interesting.

"Not at all," Professor Griffin said. "I can even arrange for you to meet the new archivist if you'd like?"

Chris must have made a face because Professor Griffin huffed a little laugh and said gently, "I know it was sudden. To be honest I'm not sure what the board was thinking, but we should at least give him a chance, hey?"

"Sure," Chris sighed, as Professor Griffin explained to his parents and aunt and uncle that the Archive's Board of Directors had already filled Aunt Elsie's position and got an appreciable number of shocked responses. "Carrie, do you want to come with?"

"I've got school stuff tomorrow," Carrie said. "Sorry, Chris, but Mrs. Hadler is paying me and I need the money."

Chapter Four

The Edgewater Maritime Archive was a concrete-and-glass building that looked depressingly industrial. It had been built for preserving delicate documents from Florida's sweltering climate and it looked it. In fact, it looked vaguely institutional. Chris wheedled his mom into dropping him off at the grim front doors at nine in the morning, and Professor Griffin let him in, munching on a carrot muffin and trying to read a letter from the Dean of Students upside down. Professor Griffin wasn't at his best in the mornings.

"Ready to pack?" he asked Chris with a strained sort of cheerfulness as they walked down the echoing hallway. "I asked custodial to leave you some boxes, and your aunt was meticulous in her organization of data. Just don't pack up any sixteenth-century charters by mistake."

"Don't worry, Professor. Aunt Elsie taught me to identify a sixteenth-century charter by sight and by feel—"

Professor Griffin raised an eyebrow.

"Which I would never do because sixteenth-century documents should always be handled with white cotton gloves," Chris continued hastily.

Professor Griffin grinned. "Spoken like a true archivist in training. Well, here we are—boxes and all." And he unlocked the door with a flourish, waving Chris inside and tipping an imaginary captain's hat. His real one was probably on the bust of Melville in his office. "Now I've got to go attend an all-college meeting about the inappropriate usage of inter-office mail to send dead birds," he said, wandering backwards down the hallway in the general direction of the front doors. "I *do* hope it wasn't Professor Delgado on a 'Rime of the

Ancient Mariner' kick again. English professors can be awfully strange," he added as he almost walked into the wall instead of the elevator.

Chris smiled, waved Professor Griffin into the elevator, then grabbed a stack of boxes from where they were piled outside the door of the office and marched inside.

Then he stopped dead on the threshold in shock. The office had been *ransacked.*

Admittedly to a casual observer it wouldn't look like anything more than a normal lived-in mess. But the books on all three of the office bookshelves were jumbled and standing at a slant, instead of perfectly perpendicular the way Aunt Elsie always kept them so the binding didn't warp. The floor rug was at an angle from the desk, which had sticky notes scattered across its surface and all of Aunt Elsie's pens jammed into a single penholder. The trashcan was beside the desk, instead of under it, and—Chris poked his head under the desk—pieces of crumpled paper and tissues were scattered where it had presumably fallen over.

And the filing cabinets, when Chris checked them, had all been rifled.

Okay, Chris said to himself. *I'm getting creeped out and concerned.* This was edging into bad-television-thriller territory, and while he might be overly imaginative Chris didn't particularly want to be bumped off for poking his nose into a criminal conspiracy. So the last thing he should do was indicate in any way that he had realized someone had been in the office before him looking for something—which standing in the dead center of his aunt's ransacked office and looking horrified was not going to accomplish.

Chris gave himself a mental shake, then went back to the hallway to grab another box and closed the door to the office with what he really hoped was a natural and innocent air. Then he pulled out his phone and took pictures of every corner of the office, even under the desk, since he figured that Carrie would blame his impression of Aunt Elsie's office on his nonexistent paranoia. *If it really* is *paranoia,* Chris thought.

In the meantime, there were Aunt Elsie's things to

pack up and then her office to search for a floorboard with a burn mark. And it was actually interesting, in a depressing kind of way, to pack up her desk and her doo-dads and whatsits and papers and such. Soothing, too. Here was Aunt Elsie's blown-glass paperweight with a sailing ship etched on it, and her other blown-glass paperweight with a sailing ship etched on it, the one with the light-up LED base, and the clay paperweight with a ship made out of macaroni that Chris had made her, and the rock paperweight with a ship painted on it that Carrie had made her—actually, Chris thought, looking into an entire box of paperweights with sailing ships on them—maybe the Kingsolver family had a paperweight problem.

He lugged the box to the growing pile next to the door and turned to the papers in the desk drawers, taking care to leave aside anything that might possibly have been the Archive's so someone could look over them later. Chris had not actually believed Professor Griffin when the man had told him that little boys who walked out of the Archive with archival property in their pockets were fed to the archive dragon, but it never hurt to be cautious. He'd already done the bookshelf—shaking every book first, in case there was a note in the pages, and checking the titles for obviously fake books—and it had been mercifully organized. And Aunt Elsie was careful and organized in general, so the collection of documents that might belong to the Archive and not Aunt Elsie, mostly internal affairs stuff, was small. Aunt Elsie never left anything even remotely fragile out of its special labeled, acid-free box, and she put little sticky notes on the folders for everything. In the end, Chris was left only with yellow legal pads covered in neat notes, professional correspondence, and three-ring binders of archive procedures. Not very interesting, but still full of Aunt Elsie's life's work, so Chris parked himself on the floor behind the desk and started filling boxes, noticing nothing unusual until he got to the bottom drawer in her desk, which stuck abominably and hardly looked like Aunt Elsie had used it in years. He had to jiggle the drawer and whack the side of the desk just to get it to open, and then sneezed at the dust that puffed into the air when the drawer squeaked open. It was half full of old folders.

Humming to himself, Chris blew some dust off a disaster-preparedness plan from 2010 and plopped it in the box, then followed it with a larger-than-normal file folder almost the exact same color as the industrial-green-painted desk. There were three even older three-ring binders stacked under it, each one taped closed with a shiny strip of duct tape and each one with the word "the" scrawled across the front in terrible cursive.

"*The* what?" Chris said to himself, prying at the duct tape with a fingernail. The tape looked newer than the binders, or at least more recently applied. "The secret to the mystery of my untimely death? The identity of the person who killed me?"

"Hello?" someone called, and Chris jumped a foot in the air.

"Aw, jeez, sorry," whoever it was said, and Chris scrambled up from the floor. He put the binders into the box *under* the file folder and the disaster-preparedness plan as he did, and desperately tried to keep a perfectly neutral face when he opened the door and recognized his mysterious visitor—by process of elimination, because Chris knew all the archivists at Edgewater by sight and didn't recognize this one—as Dr. Kevin McRae. Dr. McRae was—well, frankly he looked unfairly nice and normal. He was wearing a button-down and a tie with a pattern of palm trees, on which he was polishing his glasses. He had sad blue eyes and black curls that made him look like the young psychiatrist in the horror film who turns out to be murdering his patients because of deeply repressed childhood trauma. Chris should probably have laid off the horror films, but he'd been having trouble sleeping. Which the late-night horror movies weren't helping, actually.

"I didn't mean to startle you," McRae said, hands now in his pockets. "I heard someone in here and I wanted to lend a hand. You're Chris, right?"

Chris blinked several times, trying to decide if this was normal interest or creepy interest.

"I mean," McRae said a little too brightly, "I've seen your picture with your aunt in the director's office and I know this must be hard for you, losing Elsie so suddenly, and if there's anything I can do to make the transition easier on your family I feel I owe it to my predecessor to—"

"Chris!" Carrie's voice piped up from behind McRae. "Mom's out front with the car! Do you need help with—er, hello?" she added, stopping short and staring at McRae.

"Dr. McRae," the man in question said, shaking her hand.

"Carrie Kingsolver," Carrie said dubiously. Turning to Chris she said, "All packed up?"

"Er," said Chris, who had in fact packed up the office but had not in fact found the burn mark on the floor while doing so, "everything I could find I've packed . . . "

Carrie seemed to get his meaning, because she

nodded at him and grabbed a box. "Why don't we get this stuff in the car and then do a last sweep?" she suggested.

"Oh, good idea," Chris sighed.

"Need any help?"

"Ah, Doctor . . . "

"You could go through the pile of maybe archive stuff and weed out the definitely archive stuff?" Chris suggested. "But otherwise, we've got this."

"Oh, let me help carry things," McRae said. "And it's sometimes helpful to have an outside observer when packing—they can notice things you wouldn't."

"Sure," Carrie said sweetly, exchanging a grimace with Chris when the man's back was turned.

"What's *his* deal?" she whispered to Chris as they carried the first load of boxes out to the car. Chris shrugged. "And you didn't find it?" Carrie continued. He shook his head.

"Okay," Carrie said. "You distract him and I'll look."

But that proved easier said than done. McRae

would not leave. He wouldn't be induced to sit quietly in a corner and check the possibly-archival-papers stack, he insisted on doing a thorough sweep of the room for missing paperweights while Chris and Carrie watched him with poorly concealed terror, hoping he didn't find anything, and Carrie wasn't even able to get him tangled up in conversation with her mom. Aunt Helen was a notorious talker, possessing a nosiness that led her to terrorize new neighbors and a genuine sweetness that somehow saved her from charges of assault—but McRae managed somehow to brush off her third degree and go right back to poking his nose into everything Chris and Carrie didn't want him noticing. He kept offering to carry boxes out to the car and peering inside them as he did. It was sheer luck Chris managed to grab the last box he'd been packing for himself. He wasn't sure why, but he did not want McRae to see what was in the drawer that stuck.

Then Professor Griffin turned up with a plate of cookies he'd liberated from the college meeting and *he* wanted to help out, and if Chris and Carrie had just wanted to pack up their aunt's office it would have been as painless and comforting a day as they could have wished. Barring of course McRae, who didn't seem able to read social cues, or was too interested in Aunt Elsie's office to care. As it was, Chris and Carrie spent the whole time hoping for a chance to shoo all the adults out of the room, and the closest they came after Professor Griffin turned up with cookies was when Aunt Helen, noticing that Carrie seemed tenser than normal, came to the conclusion that Chris and Carrie were just about at the end of their tolerance for packing up their deceased aunt's things, and decided it was time to go home.

"Carrie, honey, are you coming?" she asked as she chased everyone else out the door, Professor Griffin and McRae wandering off in different directions and Chris fidgeting.

"Just give me a minute?" Carrie called from inside the office, and when Chris and his aunt peered around the door, she was sitting on the desk with her back to the door, wiping angrily at her eyes with a Kleenex. Aunt Helen sighed.

"Take as long as you need, sweetie," she said and then looked to Chris questioningly. Chris gave her a half shrug and wandered on down the hall, because he hadn't found anything in the office and if he went in now with no packing to do it was just going to hurt. Carrie came out a few minutes later with her eyes and nose red, and gave Chris such a distressed look that he knew she hadn't found the floorboard either, which really just put a cap on the whole mess. Chris went home feeling drained, didn't really pay much attention to his aunt asking him and Carrie what they wanted to do with Aunt Elsie's stuff, and was just miserable enough to hide in his bedroom and do a very small amount of crying before dinner. He suspected Carrie of going home to cry as well, and was therefore startled when she came in his window at nine in the evening with the force and determination of a small hurricane.

Chapter Five

Chris had a bedroom on the ground floor with a concrete garden bench right under his window, as he had the bedroom that looked into his mother's garden. So it wasn't at all hard to climb in his window, although if a parent caught someone there would be scolding about messing up the air conditioning and then pointed questions about what was wrong with using the front door like a civilized person. And anyway, Carrie wasn't the sort of person to climb in windows in the first place, so Chris was really very confused.

"Um," he said as Carrie stomped across his bed while he was in it. "Hello, cousin?"

"Sorry," Carrie said, "I didn't think you'd be in bed yet."

"I was checking Facebook on my phone," Chris admitted, "so I wasn't exactly asleep, but—why did you climb in my window?"

"I know, and I'm sorry about that," Carrie said, which didn't answer the question. "But I don't want my mom and dad to know that you know what I'm going to do tomorrow so I need to warn you about it—"

"Carrie!" Chris had seen her like this only once before, when she'd told a teacher the exact truth in just such a way that the boy who'd been picking on the whole second grade class got suspended. "What did you do?"

Carrie opened her mouth, apparently to angrily demand to know why Chris thought she'd *done* anything, then seemed to realize the exact circumstances and deflated a bit.

"I lost my necklace," she said.

"That . . . sucks?" Chris tried, because he wasn't sure where this was going.

"At the Archive today," Carrie explained. "And it was the one Aunt Elsie left me—"

"You lost that!?"

"Not by accident!" Carrie hissed. "It was the only one I was wearing and we needed to get back in that office!"

Chris blinked. "You *left* your locket in the office today?" he asked. Carrie nodded.

"In a desk drawer," she said. "I'm going to call Professor Griffin tomorrow and see if he'll let us come back and look for it. I'm hoping it'll give us an excuse to move the desk and the file cabinets, and I might be able to convince McRae that I really don't want help finding it on account of it being so personal and me being so embarrassed."

"I don't know if that will stop him," Chris said. "He's kinda creepy. You don't think he knows something about what happened to Aunt Elsie, do you?"

"Oh, probably!" Carrie said. "He sure seems interested in us, and Aunt Elsie, and her office—"

"Which is going to be *his* office soon," Chris pointed out.

"I know," Carrie said glumly, and they sat side by side in the dark, wondering if they'd bitten off more than they could chew.

"Well, today is a Thursday," Chris said finally. "And the Archive is closed for the next three days because the person who used to come in on the weekends is gone, so we have the weekend to plan."

"And Monday is a grace period," Carrie added. "Because McRae has to go up to his old office on Monday and get the last of his things." When Chris looked confused she rolled her eyes and added, "He told me *allll* about it while he was helping me carry a box out to the car. I have no clue what he wants but it is totally not Aunt Elsie's job."

"Great," Chris sighed. "So we still haven't found the box or even the floorboard, you had to lose your locket, and we have no idea what the deal is with McRae."

"An excellent summary," Carrie said, turning reluctantly to the window. "Not that we—actually—"

"What?"

"Oooooooohhhh!" Carrie breathed. A delighted smile broke across her face.

"Carrie, what?" Chris asked. That smile of delighted plotting never, ever boded well.

"I might possibly be able to do something about McRae," Carrie said sweetly, and scrambled out the window, through the backyard, and over the fence, leaving behind her a very puzzled and alarmed cousin.

X X X

Carrie did not pop out of the woodwork the next morning, despite the vaguely panicked impression Chris woke up with as a result of a series of dreams about cars exploding and Carrie dressed as a mobster telling him that "McRae's been taken care of." It took him some time to remember that she was working at the school until noon and did not own anything with pinstripes. Chris spent the morning eating cornflakes and watching a television special on Bigfoot, turned the television off violently when a car restoration show came on, and then gave up and did all his chores except the mail, which he was in the middle of sorting when Carrie finally did call him.

"Chris," she said, "how do you feel about terrible action movies?"

"Weren't we going to . . . ?" Chris trailed off significantly as his mom wandered past, looking surprised that he'd already done a load of laundry. He wasn't sure if they had been planning to do something, but he *was* sure that an action movie wasn't going to help them deal with Dr. McRae.

Unless it was an action movie about mobsters and Carrie really was planning to sink the man into the harbor wearing concrete overshoes and needed to watch a movie for research, but Chris didn't think his subconscious was that accurate.

"This will help," Carrie said. "I'm ninety-five-point-nine percent sure."

"Um," Chris said, wondering at the point nine. "Sure. Are you coming by or should I meet you there?"

"No!" Carrie said. "Chris, we're coming to get you in, like, half an hour. Do not still have your pajamas on!"

Then she hung up, leaving Chris to slowly realize that she'd said "we" instead of "I" and that he was, in fact, still in his pajamas.

X X X

There were two people in the car when Carrie swung by to pick him up. One of them of course was Carrie, looking cheerful and wearing yellow and demonstrating that Mrs. Hadler still had not eaten her. Chris was always slightly afraid that she would, and had probably read *The Librarian from the Black Lagoon* at an impressionable age, because Mrs. Hadler wasn't even a librarian.

The other person in the car was a girl the same age as Chris and Carrie, with her long dark hair caught up in a ponytail and a pair of strangely familiar sunglasses snagged in her collar. Her eyes were a bright and vivid blue and she was very nearly the prettiest person Chris had ever seen. She was also weirdly familiar, as though he'd seen her in passing a long time ago and never caught her name, and Chris found himself staring, trying to remember where he had seen her, trying to force her name onto the tip of his tongue. She'd been, not sad, but grave . . . wait. She was the girl from the funeral! His pulse suddenly racing from the shock of seeing a mystery up close and personal, Chris realized that he was frozen halfway into the backseat, staring. He gave himself a stern shake and scrambled into the back.

"Hey," he said, giving Carrie a desperately questioning look and scrabbling around for the seatbelt.

"Heya," Carrie chirped, bright and sing-song. "Maddison, this is my cousin Chris."

"Hi," the newly introduced Maddison said, offering Chris her hand. "Nice to meet you."

"Chris," Carrie said, "this is Maddison, she's new

in town and she's been working in the office with me. Her dad's the new archivist at Edgewater."

The world didn't exactly stutter to a halt, but Chris felt as though his stomach switched dimensions for a second.

"Oh," he said, uncomfortably aware that his voice started out an octave higher than normal and then took a swan dive. "Dr. McRae?"

"He's my dad," Maddison agreed wryly, with a self-deprecating sweep of her hands. "Maddison McRae, at your service. I'm shamelessly exploiting your cousin's good nature."

"It's apparently hard to make friends in a new area when school is closed for the summer," Carrie said. "I mean, unless you want to become best buddies with Mrs. Hadler—"

"I like her," Maddison said, chewing on the strap on her sunglasses. "She's fierce."

"And terrifying," Chris added, still trying to deal with the dizzy heat haze that was swimming in his vision whenever he looked at Maddison. She was just so incredibly pretty. And funny, even though he'd only known her for a few minutes. And—oh no . . .

Carrie, blissfully unaware of her cousin's sudden revelation that he had a crush on the daughter of the villain of the piece, added to his mortification by saying, "Well, if you're Chris, Mrs. Hadler's the devil walking among us. He tried to pass off a fake absence note in third grade and she caught him."

"Carrie," Chris protested, because it had been years and nobody in the family would let him live that down. Also now Maddison was *looking at him.*

It wasn't as though Chris had never had a crush on someone before; he'd pined for Lindsey Ipcress from first grade all the way through eighth, when her family suddenly moved to Wisconsin over winter break. And he'd actually asked Nancy Brewer to the spring formal last year. It was just that something in his head bounced up on springs when he saw Maddison, and he felt that he wanted nothing more than to talk to her forever but also that he'd melt into a puddle if she looked at him too long.

"Oh my gosh, what happened?" Maddison asked, turning all the way around in her seat to stare at him. Chris tried furiously to be cool and not melt, because it felt like he had a giant neon "I Have a Crush on You" sign flashing over his head. "Did she turn into her secret dragon form and eat you?"

"She . . . called my parents, and I got detention, and then she graded my technique and execution," Chris said, forcing himself to meet Maddison's eyes and not blush *too* much. Maybe he should be thankful they were talking about something embarrassing, it gave him an excuse to turn red.

"Also," Carrie said, "she told him he had a great future ahead of him as a counterfeiter. Chris always leaves that part out to garner more sympathy."

"Good for you," Maddison said. "Counterfeiting's a useful skill, not that I would know or anything."

"Heh," Chris managed. "Me neither. One try, and then I was scared straight!" Then he realized that he had just insulted her compliment, unless she'd meant it ironically, which he couldn't tell, and—oh this was a disaster.

"Ah-hem," Carrie added, making both Chris and Maddison jump, and realize that she was already leaning against the side of the car. Which she had parked in the parking lot of the movie theater at some point while Chris was shooting himself in the foot. "We're here, by the way," Carrie said, unfairly amused. Then she opened the door for Maddison while Chris was still fumbling with his seatbelt.

The movie, presumably picked by Carrie because it was conveniently playing just after she and Maddison got off work—she appeared to want to make friends—was called *Space Nazis at Roswell.* Almost the only good thing about the movie was the convenient timing. It was a movie about Nazis fighting aliens in the 1950s in New Mexico and there were a dozen confusing plot holes and a strangely violent subplot involving llamas. And all but one of the main characters died in the third act, preceding the unexpected reveal that the nuclear launch codes had in fact been stolen by Sasquatch.

Chris was particularly confused because there had been no mention of a Sasquatch in the movie until the last act, although Maddison had innocently parked herself in the seat beside him and asked if he wanted some of her popcorn and his sudden crush had made concentration so difficult he could well have missed it.

"Actually," Maddison said when he brought the subject up over pizza in Carrie's living room—the unexpected Sasquatch, not the unexpected crush—because Carrie invited Maddison over for takeout and Chris was suffering for conversation topics, "when they find the footage of Fritz sneaking into the bunker it's shot like the Patterson tape."

"The what?"

"Most famous film footage of Bigfoot," Maddison said, gesturing with a slice. Seeing Carrie's quizzical look she shrugged and added, "It's cryptozoology and folklore, I think it's fun. You can find it weird if you want."

"Believe me, we're both a lot weirder," Chris said,

googling the Patterson tape. "Wow, this is shaky—oh, I see what you mean."

"It looks like a person in a gorilla suit," Carrie said, peering over his shoulder.

"Many people agree with you," Maddison said gravely through a mouthful of pizza.

"Anyway, Bigfoot? Aliens?" Carrie asked.

"You caught that," Maddison said.

"I guessed," Carrie admitted. "Nobody mutters about 'grays don't do that' and 'that is *not* the hollow earth theory' unless they know a little something about aliens."

"Yeah," Maddison sighed, poking her pizza to avoid looking at them. "It's just a hobby. I'm the kid of a history professor and an art gallery manager. Developing an interest in the otherworldly was self-defense. It keeps people from trying to talk to me at regional history conferences." Chris manfully suppressed an irritated look at the mention of Maddison's father but apparently wasn't fast enough, because Maddison saw him and blew out another sigh.

"See, there's my dad, making things complicated again."

"It really wasn't—" Chris started.

"It's not your dad," Carrie said. "It's that he took our aunt's job so suddenly . . . "

"I know," Maddison said. "I don't know why he did, either. I mean, they'd asked him if he would think of coming in and consulting occasionally on this lost mission in a national park project—he teaches American history but his specialty was early Spanish colonization of the Americas—and he said no like three times, but then they gave him first priority when the whole post was open and he took it."

"Was the pay better?" Chris asked.

"I think it's the same," Maddison said. "He bounced around a bit when I was little so he didn't have tenure, and it wasn't a locked-in position or anything, but Mom runs an art gallery and we aren't desperate for money. Dad just came home one evening and said 'we're moving.' It's been weird."

"Tell me about it," Chris said.

"Oh," Maddison said. "I'm so sorry, that was rude, me complaining about having to *move.*"

"It really isn't your fault," Carrie said. "It was an accident, and you've been more than kind, and the strange things our parents do shouldn't reflect on us."

"I hope so," Maddison said. "Dad's been acting squirrely. And he insisted we go to your aunt's funeral, did you notice?"

"I thought I recognized you," Chris admitted.

"Our moving truck hadn't even made it to the house yet," Maddison said. "Mom and I had to stop at a department store just to get something black to wear, but Dad insisted that we go. He claims it was only respectful, but I just think it was tasteless, and I know it made Mom furious. Plus, when the moving truck *did* get to the house we were at the funeral, and all the basement boxes ended up in the attic." She paused. "Did your aunt, I don't know . . . know any Kevin McRaes?"

"Not that I know of," Chris said. "The name isn't at all familiar."

“Huh,” Maddison said.

“Did your dad know any Elsie Kingsolvers?” Chris asked.

“No,” Maddison said. “I think I’d remember a name like Kingsolver. I just wondered—I mean, if they had known each other and then had a falling out—it might explain something?”

“As far as I know there’s nothing,” Chris said. Carrie was spinning the ring on her finger to avoid looking at either Maddison or Chris, but for what reason Chris didn’t know.

“It’s a mystery,” she said finally, looking up and breaking the slowly gathering tension as she did so. “So! Maddison—how do you like the neighborhood?”

It was a transparent attempt to change the subject but Maddison seized it.

“Well, the first and only local event I’ve been to was a funeral,” she said, but she was smiling a little. “There don’t seem to be many kids my own age around, and my Dad is going around muttering about sixteenth-century charters.”

"That's more or less to be expected," Carrie said, getting up and gathering the now-empty pizza box and the discarded paper plates. "Almost everyone we know is either on vacation or away at camp right now, in order to avoid the tourists."

"Or helping their cousin work a lobster boat in Maine," Chris grumbled, and Carrie whacked him on the head with the pizza box.

"Who's lobstering?" Maddison asked.

"Chris's best friend Jacob," Carrie said. "And my friend Sadie. We've both been left for a lobster, or in my case a chance to get loads of practice piloting a boat. It's just me and Chris until the last week of July."

"Can I join you?" Maddison asked. "Otherwise I'll spend the whole summer reading books about local ghosts and trying to research the Bermuda Triangle. And looking forward to the weekly Bigfoot documentaries on TV."

Chris gave Carrie a meaningful look, because she was perpetually leaving Bigfoot documentaries on in the background, but Carrie just ignored him.

"Sure," she said. "Although I should warn you we were basically going to watch a show about finding ghosts and argue about it all day Sunday."

x x x

Chris and Carrie had a very strange relationship with television shows about "experts" hunting mythological creatures or doing overly scripted archeology, and they both knew it. It was a product of their fathers' joint aversion. Robby and Brian Kingsolver were both violently opposed to that sort of show, but not, as far as their kids could determine, for moral or artistic reasons. They simply refused to watch anything on any channel that was about finding Bigfoot or Atlantis, and when asked for a reason, complained about believability.

Chris actually thought the shows were interesting, Carrie seemed to find them amusing on a comic level, and neither of their mothers cared. Except Aunt

Helen, who had to avoid any television with rapidly flashing lights because she got migraines.

What Aunt Elsie had thought of the Great Kingsolver Television Debacle nobody knew, because she didn't have a television. Why Robby and Brian Kingsolver had such an aversion had never been clear; most of the family treated it as an amusing quirk and neither Chris's uncle nor his dad were interested in explaining, preferring instead to watch six hours of cat shows or accidently catch the fruit salad on fire rather than watch one episode of *Treasure Hunters*. Chris's dad had difficulties cooking.

Maddison left not long after agreeing that ghosts were better than loneliness, because her mom was on her way home from work and could pick her up. Chris waited until the car had pulled all the way out of the drive to collapse to the couch, dizzy with suppressed feeling.

"You invited—" he started.

"She'd been helping me sort student records since last Monday." Carrie's eyes were dancing with amusement.

"But you didn't—"

"I knew she was familiar but I couldn't place her until I met her dad the other day."

"So you—"

"Invited her to the movies with us, yes."

"And I—"

"Have the world's biggest crush!" Carrie gasped, and burst out laughing. Chris scowled at her. Carrie continued to laugh, a little hysterically, and finally sat down on the couch hiccupping with giggles.

Chris gave her his most plaintive and woeful expression and she finally subsided, more or less.

"Sorry," she said. "It's been a long week and . . . *your face*!"

"She's just . . . " Chris tried, and then couldn't think of an appropriate adjective and gave up. "And her dad may be out to kill and eat all of us . . . "

"Leaving aside the question of just *what* you've been watching on television," Carrie said, "I don't think Maddison knows any more than we do."

"I think we may know a lot more than she does," Chris said. "I mean I think I do—you don't think that she—"

"No, I don't think she knows anything at all about this mess," Carrie said. "Otherwise I don't think she'd have asked us if our aunt knew her dad." She stopped. "Do you think?"

"It doesn't seem likely," Chris said. "She never even mentioned him to us, and none of our parents recognized his name when the professor mentioned it."

"Then why go to the funeral?"

"To scope out the lay of the land?"

"Now there's a scary thought."

Chris began digging his shoes out from under the couch. "I like her, though," he said to the cushions, not trusting himself with face-to-face at the moment. Carrie smacked him lightly on the arm anyway, but all she said was, “Yeah, I liked her too. That’s why I offered to pick her up on my way to work tomorrow.”

“You’re trying to kill me,” Chris groaned.

Chapter Six

Carrie called Professor Griffin and asked him if she could come by the Archive and look through her aunt's old office for her missing necklace that evening. She did the deception in stages; first tearing the house apart "looking" for the necklace; then having a worried conversation with her parents in which they actually encouraged her to call the Archive; and then finally spilling the whole story to the professor over the phone. He was nicely sympathetic. Carrie told Chris as much at ten that night, as she was climbing in his bedroom window again.

"Next time," Chris said as she landed hard on the

edge of his bed and managed to pull off most of his sheets, "*I* climb in *your* bedroom window like some demented Santa Claus."

"Santa goes down chimneys," Carrie pointed out. "I got us back in the Archive, by the way," she added, as Chris grumbled that Santa had to enter somewhere when the house had no chimney, so why wouldn't the window be the most logical alternative? Then he registered what else she'd said.

"Oh, what did Professor Griffin finally say?"

"Well," Carrie said, bouncing slightly on the bed and kicking at the exercise ball, "some of McRae's boxes are already in that office."

"Oh no."

"And there's a committee meeting on Saturday so they don't want us in the building. But Professor Griffin doesn't think anybody will mind if we come in Monday evening after hours and look for it, so long as we keep McRae apprised of where we are so he isn't worried about his stuff."

"Oh *no.* Really?"

Carrie held up a hand. "So, I told him I happened to be friends with McRae's daughter and asked if it might be okay for her to be there instead of her dad, and Professor Griffin said that was totally fine."

"So all we have to do is convince Maddison to help us search an empty office for your missing necklace in the middle of the night."

"Well," Carrie said, "when you put it like *that*."

But Maddison proved to be much more enthusiastic about the idea than Chris and Carrie expected. In fact, when Carrie and Chris asked her the next day when they all reconvened, this time in Chris's living room again, she was so excited-yet-trying-to-hide-it that for a terrible moment Chris feared she was secretly planning something herself, but then she worked up the courage to admit that it was the idea of spending time in an older building after dark that was exciting. Because she wanted to look for ghosts.

"I have a camera and an EMF meter I've only ever been able to use on people's houses and this is a whole abandoned building at *night!—aaaand* you probably think I'm weird."

Chris thought she was spectacularly pretty and that the sun made her hair shine and her eyes turn an even deeper blue but his brain-to-mouth filter was still good enough that he managed not to say it.

"I do keyword cyphers for fun," he said instead, which was skating dangerously close to secret territory since Aunt Elsie had sent her last message in a keyword cypher, but was still safer than: "You have such pretty hair."

A keyword cypher, Chris explained to Maddison when she asked, was a super-simple type of encryption where a key word (hence, keyword) was used to stand for letters of the alphabet. Thus, if CHRIS was the keyword, you would first write out the keyword:

C H R I S

So that it stood in for the letters of the alphabet:

A B C D E

And then the rest of the alphabet, minus the letters that made up the keyword:

C H R I S A B D E F G J K L M N O P Q T U V W X Y Z

And then, with this standing for the regular alphabet, write out a message,

C H R I S A B D E F G J K L M N O P Q T U V W X Y Z

A B C D E F G H I J K L M N O P Q R S T U V W X Y Z

So that HELLO would now be DSJJM.

"My aunt used to call this the simplest but most effective cypher to learn," Chris told Maddison. "Because all you have to do is pick a name, which is simple enough a six-year-old can understand it. But it's plenty hard to guess the name if you don't know it, which makes it a lot trickier than something like a Caesar cypher, and so it's a good tool for teaching someone about cyphers."

"So, if I wanted to use my name?" Maddison asked.

"You would have to skip one of the Ds for it to work—like Carrie would have to leave out an R—but otherwise you'd be fine."

"Huh," Maddison said, and asked Chris a bunch of other questions about cyphers and codes, until it occurred to him to ask her what she took ghost hunting with her.

"A digital and film camera, temperature gauges, handheld recorder, and EMF meter," Maddison replied promptly. "And dad will be delighted for me to fill in, he has to be out of town until late that night. And he'll be glad to see me actually use the EMF meter, I spent two years' worth of Christmas money buying it."

"What does it even do?" Chris asked. "Detect ghosts?"

"It registers changes in electromagnetic fields," Maddison said. "The idea being, if there *is* a ghost in the area it has to be made of some type of energy, so an unusual amount of electrical energy in an area that can't be explained by normal means might indicate the presence of abnormal phenomena, like, for example—"

"A ghost," Carrie finished.

"Yep. But an EMF runs about two hundred dollars when they're cheap, so it took me forever to save up for one and I really want to use it."

× × ×

The rest of Saturday was mercifully peaceful, and Sunday went by almost without incident. Carrie hadn't been lying when she'd told Maddison the only thing they planned to do was watch bad television, and Chris was mildly surprised that Maddison still came over to Carrie's house after lunch.

"We're still moving in," she said by way of explanation. "Mom is shifting couches around and her expression was getting scary."

Carrie claimed the living room couch and waved Maddison into the seat next to her, and Chris settled on the floor with the television remote. Then they spent half an hour channel surfing and trying to convince Carrie that watching the National Chess Tournament wasn't actually that interesting, until Chris finally found a marathon of ghost-hunting shows and hid the remote from his documentary-obsessed cousin.

“What on *earth* are you three watching?” Aunt Helen asked when she wandered into the living room at noon, scaring them all half to death. Chris jumped, flailed, and fell off his perch on the back of the couch. Maddison squeaked and banged her head on the coffee table. Carrie squashed a pillow more tightly over her head and resolutely continued “watching” the show from under the decorative blankets and all the throw pillows.

On the television, someone dropped the camera and accidentally kicked it. Aunt Helen sighed, and with a pointed expression, began plucking pillows away from Carrie.

“Ghost hunting,” Chris finally said from the floor. His tailbone felt bruised and he’d spilled his cheese puffs. “I think they would actually find a ghost if they were quiet for five minutes.”

“Orbs are notoriously unreliable sources of ghost phenomena,” Maddison said, rubbing her head. “And most EMF meters are tuned to pick up household appliances, which includes cell phones and power lines!

I don't know why they're all excited about what's going to turn out to be a lens flare, or why I'm still watching this." She paused, looked sheepishly at the coffee table, and added, "You don't happen to have a bag of peas you don't want?"

"Why don't you three go in the kitchen and get some ice," Aunt Helen said. "And then maybe watch something with less screaming? There's probably even a little ice cream left," she added hopefully when nobody made signs of moving. Finally Carrie groaned dramatically and, still wrapped in a blanket and looking more like a ghost than anything they'd seen in four hours of television, wandered into the kitchen.

There was actually a lot of ice cream left, since the Professor was terrible at estimating serving sizes, so after giving Maddison a bag of chopped carrots because they were out of frozen peas, Chris and Carrie also got out the ice cream and had a small argument over toppings.

Chris didn't see any reason to put toppings on chocolate-chip ice cream. It already basically had toppings: the chocolate chips. Carrie responded by dumping half a can of honey-roasted peanuts on her bowl, because she was contrary, and possibly also insane, and—

"Uh," Maddison said, clutching her bowl protectively to her chest in the face of matching stares from Chris and Carrie, who had just then noticed the bowl of ice cream Maddison had quietly put together while Chris was trying to wrestle the peanuts away from Carrie. "Was I not supposed to use the maraschino cherries?"

"It's fine," Chris said. "But, um—"

"It's a strange combination, that's all," Carrie said hurriedly. Maddison's bowl of chocolate-chip ice cream was topped with maraschino cherries.

"It's a family tradition," Maddison said, still hugging her bowl defensively to her chest. She looked understandably unnerved by what was admittedly undue interest in her snack choices. "Mom calls it 'poor man's Cherry Garcia.'"

"It must be more widespread than we thought," Chris said. "My mom calls it the same thing."

"Mine becomes lactose intolerant whenever we have it," Carrie added. Then she grabbed the peanuts from Chris while he was distracted and made a mad dash for the living room, which only failed because Maddison was innocently standing on a corner of her blanket. They had to get out two more bags of frozen vegetables to deal with the bruises—Carrie fell flat on her face and Maddison got flung into a wall—and never did find out if the old mill was haunted.

After Maddison left Carrie told Chris he ought to go ahead and propose right this minute, since he'd never find a more perfect girl *and* she would be able to pass on the maraschino-cherry-loving gene to their offspring. Chris stared at the front door that Maddison had only just walked out of in mild horror, then reminded Carrie that some traits didn't need to be passed down, and suggested that the maraschino-cherry-loving gene might be recessive. Carrie argued that even then they'd probably have at least one kid in which it was dominant, and Aunt Helen came back from the store to find them arguing over a Punnett square.

x x x

Professor Griffin dropped off a set of keys for Chris and Carrie late Sunday afternoon, extracting their most sincere promises that they would not lose them in the process.

"And don't have any wild note-taking parties either," he said, tossing the keys back and forth and back and forth and finally at Chris. Professor Griffin was sitting in the kitchen having coffee with Chris's mom, a brave decision, as Chris's dad was cooking. "I don't want to hear that you've been a bad influence on poor Maddison."

"Who's Maddison?" Chris's mother asked. "And are you sure you won't stay for dinner, Willis? Robby is cooking."

"Honey, that's not the best way to convince him,"

Chris's dad called, as something in the oven started smoldering and the fire alarms went off.

"Maddison is Dr. McRae's daughter," Professor Griffin explained to Chris's mom as they evacuated just in front of the dense billows of smoke. "She's been working at the digitizing project up at the school with Carrie and I think they're getting to be friends."

"Oh Carrie, that's sweet of you," Chris's mom said to the newly arrived Carrie, who'd stopped halfway up the driveway with a bag of apples. She was eying the house and the smoke wafting out from the front door dubiously. Carrie was lucky enough to have parents who didn't catch the stove on fire regularly.

"What's sweet of me?" Carrie asked. "Bringing over apples to go with the pork roast that may not be happening?"

"It's just a minor fire!" Chris's dad yelled from inside the cloud of smoke. "We're still eating at five!"

"Making friends with Maddison," Professor Griffin said, completely unbothered by the interruptions. "It's very kind of you. From what I can tell Maddison could use a friend, especially considering her—er, that is, considering the stress we've all been under."

Chris and Carrie exchanged a look, Chris as sure as Carrie that the professor had started to say something completely different.

"Carrie," Professor Griffin continued, boisterous to a degree that was probably faked, "I was just telling Chris—"

"There's nothing wrong with the pork roast!" Chris's dad interrupted, holding said roast triumphantly over his head.

"No wild parties in the Archive," Professor Griffin finished, as Chris's mom steered her husband back into the kitchen very carefully, in order to prevent a repeat of the time he'd accidently dropped a roast chicken on his feet. Chris's family had never been asked to host Thanksgiving, and his dad had *still* managed to ruin the turkey twice.

"No wild parties," Chris promised the professor solemnly, jangling the keys.

Professor Griffin grinned and ducked into his car.

"I think I'll creep out while your father's trying to destroy the pork roast. I'll be back Tuesday to pick those shinies up, all right?"

"Oh," Chris's Aunt Helen said even later that evening, when she dropped by to pick up a loaf of lemon bread and fetch Carrie and gossip with Chris's dad, her first lieutenant in gossiping, "Maddison's been over at our house a few times. Bree, she's *such* a sweet kid. We ought to have the whole family over for dinner sometime."

It occurred to Chris, as his mom and aunt made plans to trap him in the house with Dr. McRae for a whole evening, that his family might be more the death of him than all the possible plotting of whatever shadowy unknown figures might be after something his aunt had known. Maddison was okay (please, please let her be okay) but her dad had—Chris got a notebook out after dinner and started a list.

Kevin McRae had taken the job at the Archive right away, despite having refused it before. He had gone to the funeral of a woman he had no apparent connection to; tried too hard to be friendly with her family, particularly her niece and nephew; searched the desk and office of the woman he replaced; and arranged a suspicious car accident to ensure she *needed* to be replaced.

"Technically we have no proof he did the last two," Carrie said when Chris showed her the list. It was Monday evening. They were sitting on Chris's front porch in the last of the sunlight, waiting for Maddison's mom to drop her off so they could go search the Archive after hours. In honor of the occasion Chris was dressed in all black, although since it was eighty degrees in the shade he had reluctantly decided not to wear a turtleneck and a beanie. He had mourned the loss of this cat-burglary staple all evening, and was suffering still further because Carrie absolutely refused to join him in attire.

Carrie was wearing a blue sundress patterned all

over with red frogs, because she had no appreciation for what was likely to be the one and only time they got close to being cat burglars. That she looked so much cooler than Chris—both in temperature and, sadly, in attractiveness—only made it more upsetting.

"Okay," Chris said, scribbling 'somebody' slantways next to the last two points. "But you see what this adds up to, right?"

"Well," Carrie said, "I see a list that is going to be *very awkward* to explain if it falls out of your snazzy black cargo pants and Maddison finds it . . . "

"Maybe I'll just go stick this in my desk," Chris said.

"Good idea," Carrie said. "And yeah, it does look suspicious. It looks like Aunt Elsie knew something somebody didn't want her to. And it looks like she was murdered to keep whatever it was a secret. And McRae's actions do suggest he's after that secret, too."

"Or that he knows we have more of the puzzle pieces," Chris said slowly. It was beginning to hit him that if Aunt Elsie had been murdered for what they were trying to find, then whoever did it was still out there and might even now be marking out two new targets. "I'll just . . . go . . . put this away . . . "

In the end he hid the list in his sock drawer, because Carrie claimed that no sane person would ever touch his socks, and Maddison seemed sane enough. Although when he got back to the front porch Maddison was on the stoop, also dressed in all black and wearing a fanny pack. Backwards.

"I'm not insane!" Maddison said, before Chris could do anything more than stop short in astonishment. "It's silly but it's super convenient," she added, doing jumping jacks. "See, no hands! If a ghost comes at me I can run like the wind without dropping anything."

"Actually, that is pretty convenient," Carrie agreed. "I just have a shoulder bag, and Chris just has a lot of pockets and a secret desire to be a cat burglar."

"Well, who doesn't?" Maddison asked.

Chapter Seven

The Edgewater Archive was even creepier than usual after hours. The parking lot it shared with the dentist next door wasn't even deserted and it still managed to look spooky, as though something large and angry was hiding behind one of the few cars still scattered across the blacktop. By unanimous and silent decision Carrie parked as close as possible to the building, and directly under one of the streetlights.

The front door groaned alarmingly when Chris turned the key in the lock and yanked it open, and the inside of the building was pitch black.

"Don't turn on the lights," Chris said when Carrie

made to flick the ones in the hallway on. She pulled a flashlight out of her purse in response, and snapped it on almost in his face. "Ow," Chris protested. "It's the Board of Directors! They're trying to save energy and if we turn lights on after hours Professor Griffin might get in trouble for letting us in here."

"Yeah, that's not foreboding at all," Carrie grumbled. She grudgingly fished another flashlight out of her bag for Chris and handed it over. "Let's just get in, find my necklace—"

"And do one sweep for ghosts?" Maddison asked hopefully. She was wearing a headlamp, and still looked enchanting. Chris was very glad it was too dark for anyone to see him blush, because he was blushing very much.

"Do one sweep for ghosts," Carrie agreed, "and then get out. Hey, Chris," she added sweetly—Chris looked at her and immediately quailed, because that was her plotting face—"maybe you and Maddison can go over the building for ghosts and meet me at the office? With any luck I'll have found my necklace by then."

"Good idea," Maddison said, pulling a video camera and a television remote out of her fanny pack. "It's always best to have more than one person on these sorts of things, for independent verification and stuff." She handed the video camera to Chris, tucked the remote back into her pack, and set about taking a preliminary temperature reading, failing to notice the silent communication Chris and Carrie were engaged in over her head.

It wasn't very good silent communication anyway. Chris gave Carrie a series of significant looks and raised eyebrows that she stubbornly refused to comprehend, and even his silent hand-flailing when she nodded angrily at Maddison as if to say, "Well, what are you waiting for?" failed to get a response. Chris was reasonably sure that Carrie was trying to help with his crush, but if this was how she defined *helping* he wondered how he would survive if she ever disliked a girlfriend.

Actually—she had not liked Lindsey Ipcress very much. Chris didn't *think* Carrie was responsible for the Ipcress family moving halfway across the country, mainly because he couldn't imagine *how* she could be responsible for the Ipcress family moving halfway across the country, but he had never been quite sure.

"I'm thinking we should start with the basement and work our way up to the third floor," Maddison said, the remote back in her hand. "Chris, you're holding the camera upside down. And this is not a television remote, it is my EMF meter," she added, effectively guessing what Chris had been too embarrassed to ask.

"Oh," Chris stammered. "Right, sorry. Are you sure we shouldn't stick together?"

"I ain't afraid of no ghosts," Carrie said.

Maddison grinned; Chris winced at the reference.

"And I want to find my necklace."

"Catch you in a bit," Maddison agreed, marching purposefully for the stairwell. Feeling like he was walking into a bad idea, Chris followed her.

"And don't let a ghost scare you into each other's arms!" Carrie called as they were just reaching the door.

Chris groaned. Maddison snorted.

"Is Carrie trying to tell us something?"

"Uh . . . " Chris trailed off. Carrie was trying to tell *him* something, all right. Mainly that she was evil, and tired of his mooning. "Um . . . " Chris tried again, holding the door open for Maddison while on autopilot. "I still don't really understand what an EMF meter does?" He could almost *feel* Carrie's disappointed scowl.

"Oh," Maddison said. "That's understandable!" She stopped on the landing and handed the EMF meter to Chris. It continued to look a lot like a television remote, with red, yellow, and green markings on one end. "Basically, if it lights up like crazy there's something weird going on with the electromagnetic field in the area," Maddison explained. "The electrical activity in the area isn't behaving normally. When ghost hunting, since most people assume ghosts have to put out some kind of energy, unusual patterns of electrical activity might be caused by ghosts."

"Maddison?" Chris said slowly. "Are a lot of so-called 'ghosts' just bad wiring?"

"Yeaaaah, pretty much," Maddison said. "But I don't think Carrie was trying to tell you to ask me about ghosts and faulty wiring . . . ?"

"Oh," Chris said. There didn't seem to be a way out. "So, I kind of, maybe, *sorta* . . . " One of Maddison's eyebrows was slowly rising into a puzzled expression, and she had crossed her arms. There was no way this could end well. " . . . haveabitofacrush," Chris finished in a rush. "It's not on you!" he added when Maddison dropped her gaze. "I mean, it is on you, but it isn't anything you did or didn't do so there's nothing to worry about, I'll just go change my name and move to Argentina and live as a hermit and—*oh I'm gonna kill her.*"

Suddenly he realized that Maddison was laughing.

"Er," said Chris.

Maddison huffed and looked him square in the face. "Are you trying to tell me you have a crush, and that the crush is on me?" she asked. She had Chris cornered against the stair railing, and he spared a brief thought to jumping over the side to avoid the awkwardness of the ensuing conversation. But the steps to the basement level were dark and the drop was far and that would be very final, unless he came back as a ghost. And if he came back as a ghost, Maddison would still believe in him enough to want to have the conversation. So, it was pretty much a terrible idea.

"I'm trying not to tell you," Chris admitted. "But it doesn't seem to be working. You can be offended if you want to, I don't mind."

"Actually I am *so* relieved," Maddison exclaimed. She was full-on smiling now, which was a good thing, Chris hoped. "You've been super nice but kind of weird this whole time. I was starting to think you were secretly a serial killer or a spy for the Russians."

"You thought I was a serial killer but you still came with me to explore an empty building in the middle of the night?" Chris asked, suddenly feeling guilty for imagining that Maddison's dad was a serial killer even if he did still halfway suspect the man of being one. He was going to feel particularly awful if he turned out to be right.

"It's eight thirty," Maddison said, "and I have two cans of mace in my super-dorky backwards fanny pack. And anyway you don't have a secret agenda. You just have a crush."

"Right," Chris agreed, now feeling even guiltier and very, very trapped. If he came out right now and admitted the truth—Maddison might push *him* over the railing.

"And, Chris," Maddison said, serious but kind at the same time, "I barely know you, and what I do know I *really* like. But I don't feel the same way about you that you feel about me." Which was what Chris had been expecting, in the back of his mind, all along. "So," Maddison continued, "if it's okay with you I'd like to be friends? And maybe we'll be more, in a little while?"

"I'd like that," Chris said, resolving to himself that as soon as possible he was going to come clean about the whole secret. Preferably after he and Carrie figured out exactly what was going on, so he could present it to Maddison as a finished indiscretion. And privately agreeing that he really wanted to get to know Maddison a little more. What kind of girl hunted ghosts with scientific precision because her father was a history professor? "Shall we go in search of ghosts?" Chris asked, offering Maddison his arm.

"I thought you'd never ask," Maddison said, grinning and taking it. "But you'd better have that video camera running at all times in case we meet one."

Sadly for the prospective of running screaming into each other's arms, Chris and Maddison did not come across a full-fledged phantom glowing green and rattling chains.

"But that's not very likely anyway," Maddison said, checking the temperature in the third-floor lounge. "I'd be happy for just a definitely unexplained cold spot, or electrical activity far beyond what you get from power lines, or a little glowing mist."

"I'd be happy if we didn't find anything," Chris admitted. Watching people look for ghosts on television was one thing, actually looking for them yourself was entirely another. The shadows kept reaching out and grabbing at him, and the idea of glowing mist was *not* appealing. He'd spent a lot of his childhood in this building, and it had never before seemed so creepy or so full of dark corners from which a ghost or shadow monster might conveniently lunge.

"Well," Maddison said, "I've been doing this for years and the scariest thing I ever saw was my aunt covered in soap suds and chasing the cat."

"Were you looking for that?"

"*Nooo*," Maddison said. "But she was really angry and it looked darn amazing with my night vision goggles."

"What about aliens?" Chris asked as another worrying thought occurred to him.

"I've never seen aliens," Maddison said. "I *have* heard strange whistling in the woods when we were visiting my grandparents in Washington—which means I could have heard a Sasquatch," she explained. "But no aliens. Why, have you ever experienced periods of lost time or bizarre dreams?"

"Uh," Chris said, thinking that while his dream

of Carrie as a mob boss was definitely bizarre it was probably not what Maddison meant. "No."

"Then I think you're fine," Maddison said. "Now, the Bermuda Triangle or a similar supernatural hotspot, that we might need to worry about."

They didn't find spooky glowing mist on the bottom floor, or the first. They didn't find any on the second floor, where Aunt Elsie's office had been and where Carrie was, either. But they *did* hear a door slam shut.

X X X

Edgewater Archives was a blocky building built for function rather than appearance, more or less resembling a box. There were utilitarian stairwells on both sides of the building and an elevator in the middle by the reception desk, and Maddison and Chris had been taking the stairs for the dual reasons that stairs were a prime ghost location and that elevators were claustrophobic and sketchy at night in deserted buildings.

They were halfway down the main hallway of the second floor when the stairwell at the opposite end of the floor slammed shut.

"What was that?" Chris asked, and then realized that Maddison was jogging lightly and noiselessly down the hall, her long black ponytail bouncing. More alarmed than he would have liked to admit and wanting very much not to be alone in the hallway, he ran as quietly as possible after her, and caught up just as she was noiselessly pushing the door open.

The stairwell was empty, and when they checked there were no suspicious cold spots or electrical activity. Chris sighed in guilty relief and Maddison sighed in disappointment and kicked lightly at a wedge of wood on the top landing.

"And sometimes the ghost is actually a doorstop that didn't hold the door very well," she said.

Chris was already a little more alarmed by all this ghost hunting than he was trying to let on. So he decided not to tell Maddison that he thought he'd heard, just as they reached the door at the top of the stairs, the click of the door at the *bottom* of the stairwell being pushed open. It was most likely his imagination, if it wasn't his imagination it was probably the wind, and Chris did not want to consider what it might be if it wasn't the wind.

"Ah, well," Maddison continued, turning around and leading the way back up the stairs. "Maybe we'll get something from the video. In the meantime, we should go help your cousin with the real reason we're here. Especially since I'm technically supposed to be making sure nobody steals my dad's paperweight collection."

"He has a paperweight collection?" Chris couldn't help asking. They were taking the stairs two at a time and the nervous prickle at the base of his neck had almost disappeared.

"Oh, yeah. And it's all octopuses."

"That's funny, because my Aunt Elsie had a giant paperweight collection that was all sailing ships—whoa."

The office looked like an obsessive-compulsive tornado had hit it.

"Sorry," Carrie said, from behind the desk she was determinedly dragging away from its long-standing spot by the window, which it had occupied since before Aunt Elsie's predecessor took the office. "There's just the tiniest space between the floor and the desk and I can't find my necklace anywhere. Maddison, I'll move it back before we leave, I promise," she added. She glanced around the room. "Er, *all* of it, that is." Carrie had pushed everything in the room that could be pushed up against the walls.

"It's totally fine," Maddison said, hurrying over and tucking her EMF meter in her fanny pack as she did. "Here, let me help you with that."

Chris stayed where he was, frozen. He'd recognized the note of real hysteria in Carrie's voice when she'd said that she couldn't find the necklace, and a terrible thought was sending ice down his spine.

"You don't remember where you had it last?" he asked nervously.

"I *thought* it must have fallen in one of the desk drawers," Carrie said, and the worried look she gave him was proof enough. "But I can't find it *anywhere.*"

Chris swallowed in a vain attempt to squash the metallic taste of panic in his mouth. Between the time Carrie had left the necklace in the office on Thursday and the time they came back to "search" for it, someone else had searched the office and taken the necklace, and this was very, very bad.

"Don't worry," Maddison said, innocent of the real situation and trying to reassure Carrie nonetheless. "If it's here we'll find it." She gave the desk a final push and with a horrible groan it moved a reluctant couple of feet. "Whoa," she added. "*That's* a weird mark."

Chris took a deep breath and fought off the hysterical urge to giggle at what had finally been found under the desk. They may have lost Carrie's necklace—the only tangible thing Aunt Elsie had given Carrie, and the only thing she had to remember her by—but they had at last found the scorch mark. And Maddison was right. The long-looked-for scorch mark, now discovered under the desk drawers, was indeed weird. It looked as if someone had branded the floor with a four-pointed star.

"The four points of a compass," Carrie said to herself, dropping to her knees and rapping on the scorch mark. She'd rallied slightly better than Chris, despite being the one the necklace belonged to. "Hey! This sounds *hollow,*" she added, convincingly surprised.

"Points of a compass?" Chris asked, dropping to the floor next to Carrie.

"*Hollow*?" Maddison asked. She joined Chris and Carrie. "Well, should we open it?"

"I—the four points make me think of the four points of a compass," Carrie explained. "I don't know why. And I don't think it could hurt anything if we pulled the board up and saw if there was anything inside. Especially if we inform the proper authorities after we do."

And so saying, Carrie dug her fingernails into the crack between the scorched board and the next and tugged. There was a creak and groan from the wood, and then with a puff of dust and stale air the floorboard came up. Inside was a small hollow, hacked into the insulation and wreathed with wires and bracketed by two pipes. Nestled inside the hollow was a wooden box about half the size of a regular shoe box.

"Careful!" Carrie hissed as Chris gently reached down and tugged it out. She was clutching the floorboard to her chest protectively. "There might be exposed wires or—"

"Nah," Maddison said, "don't worry about that, I left my EMF meter on. No electricity *or* ghosts."

"Got it," Chris said, blowing insulation dust off the lid and then scrubbing the rest off on his pants. Without the dusty covering, the box proved to be a warm, reddish wood, trimmed on the corners with brass and embellished on the top with an etched brass plate depicting a Spanish galleon in full sail on a rough sea. The initials E.K. were inserted cleverly into the billows in the storm clouds.

Maddison traced the initials with a finger. "Somehow I think this belongs to your family."

"E.K.," Chris said. "Aunt Elsie, what are you trying to tell us?"

"Always be on the lookout for secret compartments?" Maddison suggested. "Carrie, this is awesome but I'm not seeing your necklace anywhere."

"I know," Carrie said. "I'm absolutely certain that I had it when I walked in here last week, and I could have sworn that I lost it in here while I was helping Chris carry boxes, but I've searched every inch of this office and it's just not here."

"Maybe somebody found it later and turned it in to the lost and found?" Chris suggested.

"I checked with the front desk about that before I asked the professor if we could search the office," Carrie said. "As of last Friday there hadn't been a necklace matching that description turned in."

"Checked your pockets?" Maddison asked a bit desperately.

"Yup."

"Checked this box?"

"Can't," Chris said, flicking ineffectually at the

lid. "It seems to be locked." Which was a whole new problem to deal with, because Aunt Elsie hadn't left them a key.

"I can ask my dad to check the box of archive papers for a necklace," Maddison offered, "in case it got mixed in with them, or—unless you don't want me to?"

"No, Maddison, that would be great," Carrie said. "You really don't even have to do that much, if it isn't here then it might just be lost forever." She sighed. "I think we should probably put the desk back where it was, and you should check your dad's boxes for the sake of thoroughness."

"Right," Maddison said. "It is getting pretty late, and I wanted to be home in time to see my dad before he goes to bed."

Chapter Eight

MOVING THE DESK BACK AND TIDYING THE THINGS Carrie had shifted took barely five minutes, and then they were locking up the office and tiptoeing down the stairs, Carrie tucking the box in her shoulder bag as they went. There shouldn't have been a need to tiptoe, but it was late, and Chris, at least, was beginning to feel drained as the adrenaline from chasing ghosts and actually losing the necklace and then finally finding the box faded.

Even Maddison—who presumably had had a much less stressful evening than Chris or Carrie because the stakes were so much lower for her—looked a little beat. Her customary bounce was so subdued it hardly made her ponytail sway. And the eerie feeling that they weren't alone had returned tenfold.

"Lucky you found that box, though," Maddison said as they trooped tiredly down the stairs. "Otherwise it might have been hidden away forever."

"Aunt Elsie liked doing stuff like that," Chris offered. They were crossing the front lobby, and their footsteps echoed loudly in the higher-ceilinged room. Maddison was glancing surreptitiously at her EMF meter. "She loved puzzles too, all kinds of codes—I'll bet there's some complicated code needed to open the lock on that box."

"Or you could just gently take it apart at the seams and then put it back together," Maddison suggested.

"Well, yeah," Chris agreed, "but where's the fun in that?" He paused at the front door to lock up, Carrie shifting uneasily from foot to foot. "And anyway," Chris continued, more to chase away the prickle on the back of his neck than anything else, "Aunt Elsie likely gave the key to someone in the family a long time ago, disguised as a letter or a movie ticket or a bottle of grape soda . . . ”

“I’m still annoyed at you for that spilled bottle of grape soda,” Carrie said.

“It’s a long story,” Chris admitted to Maddison, who looked like she wanted to ask but was afraid she’d regret it. “And Carrie might kill you if I told you.”

“It was a white dress, Chris,” Carrie said, leading the way to the parking lot. She unlocked the car when they were still a few feet out, and it somehow seemed a necessary precaution. “A *new* white dress.”

“I said I was sorry!” The streetlight they had parked under was, by some piece of cosmic irony, the only one that was out, and Chris kicked it as he passed it. The creeping feeling of eyes on the back of his neck wasn’t going away, and it felt like an insult for the streetlight to stand there, tall and proud and not doing its job.

It was nearly midnight, and the night had cooled as the stars peeked out and a warm wind blew in. The parking lot was almost empty—there was a nondescript gray car parked near the entrance to the dentist’s office—and the working streetlights bathed it in dirty yellow light. This did nothing for Chris's strange feeling of creeping dread, which did not go away as they pulled out of the parking lot and he almost ran a red light. Actually, Chris probably shouldn't have been driving while feeling this unsettled, but the family rule was that if Carrie drove one way, Chris drove back.

"Is something wrong?" Carrie asked.

"I don't think so," Chris admitted. "But the hairs on the back of my neck have been standing up all night."

There was a foreboding moment of silence while Carrie and Maddison exchanged a worried look. And, Chris wondered to himself, how had they developed shared worried looks already? But more to the point, why had they not included him in the development?

"Now that you mention it . . . " Carrie said. "There's been this prickle on my scalp all night."

"Me too," Maddison said.

Chris didn't say anything, but he didn't have to.

"Did you guys bring a ghost home?" Carrie asked, only half joking.

"No," Maddison said. "It doesn't work that way. Ghosts are generally tied to one place, and that place is usually where they died—and although I never look up the history of a place before I go ghost hunting, it's pretty unlikely anyone ever died horribly in the Archive. And anyway, the place was quiet as the grave." She winced at her own choice of words. "I mean, we didn't see or detect a thing. Um. Unless—"

"Unless what?" Carrie asked.

"We might have *heard* a ghost," Chris offered. "We heard that door slam, remember?"

"Do ghosts slam doors?" Carrie asked.

"Sometimes," Maddison said. "But there was no evidence to suggest it wasn't the door jamb coming loose."

"Except," Carrie said slowly, "that Chris and I know the janitor at the Archive and Mr. Fitzgerald hammers those things in so tightly it takes three people to pry them out sometimes. The door *might* swing loose, but it would be a pretty odd coincidence."

"See, this is why I usually investigate first and *then* look up the history of the place," Maddison said. "No preconceived notions of what's supposed to happen. It just doesn't usually end up *verifying* a ghost."

"So, now I'm thinking we really did almost catch a ghost," Chris said. "And tonight just got a whole lot scarier, somehow."

"What if," Maddison started, then she bit her lip and stopped.

"What if what?" Carrie asked.

"What if it wasn't a ghost?" Maddison said slowly. "Isn't someone watching you supposed to make the hairs on the back of your neck stand up—*Chris, move*!!"

The next few moments were forever a blur in Chris's mind. He'd taken a driver's education class, and been properly unimpressed by the instructor's insistence that crashes happen in seconds and when you least expect them, and now, well. He knew that he *registered,* on some level, that there was a car about to crash into him, and that he acted on panicked instinct he hadn't known he had, but how long it took and, for example, who screamed and who didn't, all got lost in a moment of white noise and then his brain decided he didn't need the memory.

He realized much later, after the adrenaline wore off, that they were lucky they'd been on a side street after dark. It meant that there were plenty of dark alleys for someone to come speeding out of unexpectedly, but it also meant that when Chris slammed on the gas pedal harder than he'd ever done in his life there was nobody in front of them to run into. The car that had come roaring out of the mouth of the alley missed crashing into them by inches—in fact it scraped the back bumper it was so close—before cutting its lights and speeding away.

"That was too close!" Maddison said, rolling the window down and leaning halfway out, the better to snap a picture of the fast-receding car. Chris pulled over and put the car he was driving in park, because he didn't trust himself behind the wheel at the moment. "They almost hit us!" he gasped.

"They would have hit us if you hadn't noticed them," Carrie gasped. "What warned you they were there?"

Chris was staring at the dashboard clock, still slightly frozen in shock and wondering if this was what it felt like in the aftermath of an alien abduction. He'd lost a minute or two and wasn't sure what he'd done in the interim.

"I—I saw headlights," Maddison said, "unexpectedly. I just thought they weren't paying attention. I didn't expect—" She swallowed. "That car was aiming for us, wasn't it?"

For a half second, Chris considered lying, but there didn't seem to be a point. "I think they were," he said.

"It was the car from the parking lot," Carrie added.

"But why?" Maddison wailed. "Someone just tried to *kill* us! There isn't a point to all this!"

Chris looked at Carrie, who shrugged, put an arm around Maddison's shoulders, and said, "We don't know, either. But, well, ever since Aunt Elsie died, things have been weird."

"Weird how?" Maddison asked.

"Sketchy people at her funeral," Carrie said.

"Not your family," Chris added, and Maddison half smiled.

"That prickling feeling at the back of your neck," Carrie continued. "And the Archive Board of Directors replacing her super-fast . . . "

"And there was something off about the police report," Maddison added. Chris stared. "Dad—Dad had a copy," she added, which didn't really explain anything. "I think he's more worried about the Archive than he's letting on."

"Something might be . . . off, about how our aunt died," Carrie admitted. "And it's possible someone's been following us ever since we packed up our aunt's things at the Archive. But I had no idea someone would try to kill any of us."

"The absolute last thing we wanted was to put you in danger," Chris added, wondering in the meantime if McRae was responsible, and if so, *had he known his daughter was in the car*?

"She was pushed off the road," Maddison said faintly. It took a second for Chris to realize that she was talking about Aunt Elsie. "Just like we almost were. So then the creeping feeling that we were being watched . . . ?"

"Oh ick, somebody *was* watching us!" Carrie exclaimed. "Probably the same person who went after Aunt Elsie—oh." She froze. "I thought it seemed familiar." When Chris and Maddison just blinked at her she swallowed hard and elaborated. "The—the car that almost hit us. I can't be certain, but it looked familiar. I think—I think it might have been the same car that followed Chris and me home the other day."

"Okay," Maddison said. "Okay, I'm okay." She didn't *sound* okay. "Do you mind just dropping me off at home? This has been a long night."

"Sure," Chris said.

"And be careful about alleys?" Maddison added.

"Very careful," Chris agreed, and not at all

facetiously. But the rest of the drive passed perfectly quietly. There were no cars sitting in alleys with their lights off, or following uncomfortably close. There were no cars acting suspicious at all.

"They must have accidentally turned the headlights on when they started toward us," Maddison said quietly, finally breaking their still-stunned silence.

"And I'll bet that car you thought was following us last Friday *was* following us," Carrie said to Chris, who shuddered.

Maddison's father was at the door to meet her when they dropped her off. He was concerned by how late it was and by the fact that Maddison was pale and still shaking slightly, which was understandable for someone who had just survived a murder attempt, but less understandable for someone who had been helping a friend search for a piece of jewelry. He did not look like he had just tried to cause a fatal car crash, unless he was in the habit of doing so in his pajamas.

"He could have doubled back," Chris said to Carrie

as he pulled into his driveway ten minutes later. "If you had only let me get out and feel the hood of his car—"

"Because Maddison wouldn't have found that suspicious at all," Carrie sighed. "Chris, either this incident proves that Kevin McRae had nothing to do with Aunt Elsie's death, or it proves that he is entirely willing to sacrifice his daughter for the sake of whatever is in this box. Either way, what is the last thing we should do?"

"Suggest in any way that we suspect him or know anything about Aunt Elsie's secrets?"

"Yup," Carrie said. Chris and Carrie shared a sigh. Then they climbed out of the car, locked it, and trooped inside Chris's house, trying hard to act casual and as if they hadn't found anything interesting at all in the office. The house was silent, and empty of all but the occasional bubbling of Chris's dad's aquarium. His parents were at a square-dancing competition and wouldn't get back until the early morning hours. Possibly later if they made it to the final round.

This was, Chris thought with a pang, exactly the sort of night he used to spend with Aunt Elsie. For a few minutes, they just fidgeted around the kitchen, Carrie getting a can of soda out of the fridge and Chris absently picking at some grapes, but finally neither could take the suspense anymore.

"Well, you want to try opening the box?" Carrie asked.

Chapter Nine

They checked that all the doors and windows were locked first. There wasn't a security system to turn on, because the neighborhood was quiet and the last criminal activity in the neighborhood, if it could be called that, had been when the Randalls' son came home from college while everyone in his family was on vacation, forgot his key, and climbed in the side window, causing the next-door neighbor to call the police and report an intruder. The subsequent search for the home invader she reported to the police took nearly five hours.

So all Chris and Carrie could do, fresh off almost

being run off the road by a mysterious adversary and not sure if they had been followed home, was lock the doors and windows. Then they settled in Chris's bedroom, and Carrie pulled the mysterious box out of her bag and set it down on the desk. The bronze trimmings shone dully in the light of the single desk lamp Chris turned on, and they set about examining it.

The box proved to be securely locked and the lock was intricate: the lid was held closed by a hinged bronze latch, shaped like a spade from a deck of cards and with a finely wrought sun in the middle. It was a gorgeous piece of workmanship, even if there didn't appear to be even so much as an opening for a key and you couldn't even wedge the lid up enough to peek inside. Chris said as much, picking at the latch with a fingernail.

"There has to be a key, though," Carrie said. "Unless we go with Maddison's suggestion and take the whole thing apart, and I want to try everything else first."

"Except," Chris said, examining the bottom of the

box for the third time, "taking it to an archivist and asking for an appraisal?"

"Well no, we probably don't want to ask McRae to take a look at it, and we'd better hope Maddison doesn't think to mention this to him. Or if she does, that it doesn't register," Carrie said. "Although if worse comes to worst we might ask Dad or Uncle Robby. Or maybe the professor."

"I'm not sure you could even take it apart," Chris added. He handed the box to Carrie. "The craftsmanship on this thing is incredible. Where do you think she got it?"

"It looks old," Carrie said with a shrug, after turning the box over in her hands. "No watermark or maker's mark—"

"Maker's mark?"

"Um, the mark of the manufacturer. Sometimes they call it a maker's mark," Carrie said absently. "This is real bronze, and I have no idea how to tell the age of an etching or an engraving. But it has Aunt Elsie's initials so I'd guess it was expensive," she added. "How do you open?" she asked the box.

"Maybe," Chris suggested, laying his head down on the desk and staring at the box from his new sideways vantage point, "we should fold the letter Aunt Elsie sent me into some kind of origami key?"

"Well, she did give me a book on origami folding for my fourteenth birthday," Carrie said. "But somehow I think that's a stretch even for—"

"Wait a second," Chris interrupted her, "I think this might come off." He sat up and ran his fingers carefully over the sun decorating the latch, and he wasn't mistaken. The piece of brass was raised, just enough to suggest it was a separate piece, and what looked like decorative balls on the tips of every other ray might be holding it on. Chris pushed the small brass sun gently away from him, which caused a startling squeak of metal—and then the sun swung to the side, revealing a small oval depression fitted with a series of grooves.

"Okay," Carrie said. "We've . . . found the keyhole?"

"Yeah," Chris agreed, "but where's the key?"

"We're looking for something round, with a pattern of raised surfaces," Carrie said. She ran a finger thoughtfully across the depression. "And I'll bet it is brass, same as the lid. Drat, hang on," she added, because her phone was ringing. It was a ringtone Chris didn't recognize.

"If I were a key Aunt Elsie gave to us, how would I be disguised?" Chris asked himself, digging in his desk drawer for a notepad.

"Hi, Maddison, what's up?" Carrie asked, standing up and walking over towards the door.

"About this big," Chris said, still to himself, now sketching it out on his trusty notepad. "Probably brass, and with a raised pattern that copies the grooved pattern of the keyhole, which looks like this . . . "

"He thinks *what*?" Carrie said in the background. "Why does—oh. I—yeah, okay, we will—"

"Huh," Chris said. If you assumed a circular brass object the same size as the keyhole with markings that were the exact reverse, you got something that looked remarkably like—

"You just drew my locket," Carrie said slowly. "And that was Maddison on the phone."

Chapter Ten

Maddison was on the phone, Chris learned later, because her father had noticed how rattled she was by her recent brush with death and demanded to know how visiting an archive as a favor for a friend could leave her so shaken. Which was either a clever extra layer of ruse or more proof that Kevin McRae wasn't involved. Chris was still reserving judgement. As Maddison had no idea that her father might possibly be responsible for one murder and another attempted murder, she had proceeded to tell him the entire story.

"Even the part about my having a crush on her?" Chris wanted to know.

"Strangely, that didn't come up in the conversation," Carrie said.

Kevin McRae had reacted to Maddison's unintentionally edited version of events by exclaiming that he knew something like this would happen.

"Something like what?" Chris had asked. Carrie had told him to shut up and let her finish.

Dr. McRae had asked Maddison for a description of the car, scribbled it down in a notepad while muttering a number of rude words and that he should have known, and then told Maddison to warn her friend Carrie that she might still be in danger before dashing out the door, already on the phone to what sounded like a police detective.

Maddison was bewildered by her father's reaction. "I was expecting him to be freaked out about the whole 'car tried to run us over' part," Maddison had told Carrie, "and he was, but he *also* immediately decided it was part of a bigger plot that involved you and Chris, which, what the heck?"

"That *is* a puzzle," Carrie had said. When she

related the conversation to Chris, she had ended it with a smack to the head and the comment that, "if you don't fess up about the lost treasure ship soon she is going to hate you."

Unfortunately, the narrative of why Maddison had called Carrie at one in the morning in a panic had to wait for after the fact, because only seconds after Carrie told Chris that it had been Maddison on the phone the glass on the picture window in the kitchen shattered. The large, *ground-level* picture window in the kitchen.

Chris and Carrie froze, listening to glass tinkling and then the unmistakable sound of heavy footsteps in the house. Unless their parents had come home very early and forgotten both their keys and their common sense, there was an intruder in the house.

"Maddison was warning me that someone might try breaking into the house," Carrie whispered, casting worried glances from the open bedroom door to the desk lamp they'd turned on when they came home. Her eyes were very wide.

"Gee, ya think?" Chris hissed. Then he grabbed

the box and his notepad, yanked the loose floorboard under his desk up, and shoved them both into the resulting hole. The footsteps were coming, faster now, down the hallway, almost as loud as Chris's pounding heart. Carrie scrambled to her feet and was just at the door when a guy Chris had never seen before came barreling the last few feet down the hallway, gun in hand and heading right for them.

Actually, Chris had seen him before—it was the uncomfortable, sketchy-looking guy in sunglasses he'd seen at the funeral! Chris was frozen, but Carrie's adrenalin-fueled response was more vicious—she yelped in terror and threw herself at the door, *into the path of the gun he was raising,* slamming it closed on Sketchy Guy's arm with such force that the gun went skittering across the floor even as she screamed. Then she *stayed there,* entire body jammed against the door in an effort to keep someone three times her size from pushing it open.

"Chris," Carrie said, back against the door and all her weight keeping a scrabbling hit man—because really, what else could he be?—from throwing the door open. She had been screaming but that had stopped; now she was glacially calm and very pale in a way that suggested she was almost at the point where superhuman strength set in. "I think you should go out the window and call the police."

"And—and leave you here with a homicidal gunman?" Chris asked. "No way!"

"If you go call the police," Carrie said, panting with the effort of keeping Sketchy Guy from shoving the door open, "they might *get here* before my strength gives out!" She was skidding a little on the floor, even though she was wearing shoes. Chris cast a desperate look at the window, but his conscious won out over his sense of self-preservation and he joined Carrie at the door, lending his weight to hers. This earned him an inarticulate wail of frustration from Carrie.

"How is this helping?" she demanded.

"I can't just leave you alone with a dangerous criminal!" Chris put his shoulder to the door; it didn't help.

Sketchy Guy was stronger than Chris was, and Chris could feel his feet slipping.

"One of us needs to survive!" Carrie retorted. "Because of the *thing*!"

Chris spared a moment to marvel at his cousin's devotion to secrecy, although talking about "the thing" was still a bit of a giveaway. Nobody talked about "the thing" and meant the grocery list. They might have been talking about a radiation monster, but you couldn't hide one of those. Plus, Chris suspected Sketchy Guy had a better idea of what he was looking for than Chris and Carrie did.

There was a furious roar from the other side of the door. Apparently Sketchy Guy hadn't counted on either of them holding out this long, which was reassuring but also worrying. Chris couldn't hold out much longer, Carrie had been slipping before Chris joined her, and in fact even with their combined strength the door was inching open. Chris decided, irrelevantly, that being trapped in an action movie was a terrible experience and he'd like out now, and then suddenly had an actually passable idea.

"Carrie," he said, in an undertone, "remember how Fritz and Freda escaped from the zombie llamas?"

"What?" Carrie asked, after a terrible second where she just *stared* at him and Chris hoped desperately that she remembered the movie from Friday. Then her incredulous expression cleared and she looked faintly relieved. "Oh. Yes," she gasped, "but do you think that actually works in real life?"

"No," Chris admitted, "but if it does it might be our only chance, so on the count of three?" He did not want to know what Carrie had thought he meant about zombie llamas before she remembered the movie.

"Oh," Carrie sighed, "we'll probably die, but sure."

"One," Chris said, and braced himself against the door.

"Two—no, wait!" Carrie said, and frantically darted across the room to snag the dropped gun.

"Carrie," Chris groaned as Sketchy Guy shoved the door open far enough to get three fingers in.

Whimpering, Carrie threw her full weight at the door again—there was an anguished howl from the other side of the door—and fumbled the magazine out of the gun. She gave Chris a furious shrug when he stared at her in amazement and then she kicked the now-useless gun under the bed.

"Three," Chris said, and in a mostly synchronized move they swung away from the door. Abruptly and with no warning. Sketchy Guy went flying into the room and Chris and Carrie bolted out past him as fast as possible. As they did Chris grabbed the gym bag Sketchy Guy had dropped when he fell, on the basis that if he could do anything to thwart the man he should. Carrie slammed the door shut on her way out and then hurled the small but solid side table across the doorway, which, from the sound of it, caught Sketchy Guy across the mid-thigh as he lunged after them. It served to slow him down but did not, unfortunately, stop him.

The Kingsolver residence was not very big and mostly open plan. Chris had a room in the middle of the house; to get to the door they had to cross the living room, which, when you were fleeing a large, sketchy man who may have had more than one gun, was much farther away than it had ever seemed before. And Chris was not much of a runner. He'd never actually failed gym class but he tripped over absolutely everything. It would have been just exactly Chris's luck to do something like trip painfully over the coffee table on his way towards the front door, but what he had not expected to do was collide with an armed police officer three steps from the front door. Which was in fact what happened. Carrie, who'd been a hair behind him, skidded to a stop and tripped, and actually did crack her head painfully on the side table.

Someone other than the startled man in Kevlar Chris had just flattened yelled, "Freeze!" over his head, and there was a magnificent thump, as though Sketchy Guy had tried to stop and instead collided with the ottoman. Chris gingerly picked himself off the police officer, handing over the gym bag as he did, and discovered that Sketchy Guy had in fact tripped over the decorative treasure chest parked conveniently next to the couch. The Kingsolver family had at least six *legitimate* seafarers in its tree, not including all the pirates, so a decorative style that tended towards nautical was the natural result of various inheritances. So it wasn't as odd as it might have been for there to be a sea chest in the living room. If the chase had happened in Carrie's house, they may have been rescued by the old diving suit that decorated theirs. This could have been even more interesting given the fact that the old diving suit had a tendency to fall over unexpectedly, making a magnificent crash; Chris's dad insisted it was haunted. But then, Chris's dad thought a lot of things were haunted.

A lot of police officers were now pushing their way through the door, and like a dandelion or a telemarketer popping up out of nowhere when least expected or wanted, Dr. Kevin McRae appeared.

"Okay," said the man in the suit holding the badge, seven minutes and a lot of yelling later. "Is there actually a coherent explanation for any of this?"

Nobody volunteered one. The obviously-a-police-detective pinched the bridge of his nose and muttered something that sounded like, "Why do I always get the crazy ones?"

It took three hours to take everyone's statements and give the police a complete idea of what had happened, and even then Chris suspected that not a single person had told the entire truth to Detective Hermann, the previously mentioned man in the suit with the badge. Detective Hermann was an older man with a bushy white mustache and an air of resigned bewilderment that made you want to reassure him that you knew what you were doing, and the unfortunate first name of Melville, which he admitted immediately upon introducing himself. He claimed it was to get the awkwardness out of the way quickly, but it occurred to Chris at the two-hour mark that the detective was getting everyone to underestimate him and to confide in him all in one fell swoop, and his respect for the man increased tremendously.

Chris's parents arrived home in the middle of hour three. It was hard to say who was more alarmed: Robby and Bree Kingsolver, who came home to a house full of police officers, or the officer watching the door, who opened it to a middle-aged couple wearing matching blue-sequined cowboy hats and clutching a second-place ribbon. Detective Hermann stared at their square-dancing outfits for a long moment and then visibly resigned himself to a case that made no sense.

Sketchy Guy, whose name proved to be Cliff Dodson, was almost painfully chatty. He readily admitted to ransacking Elsie's office, breaking into the Kingsolver's house, and being behind the wheel of the car that drove Elsie off the road, and seemed strangely averse to asking for a lawyer or to the common courtesy of confessing to murder away from the family of the victim. That his name really was Cliff Dodson Chris doubted. Of his insistence that he had acted alone, as he claimed multiple times and with increasing insistence, Chris had even more serious doubts. Cliff's insistence that he'd gone after Aunt Elsie because she was in charge of a collection of gold artifacts that he believed he had prior claim to also didn't ring true. Aunt Elsie had seldom, if ever, handled the few artifacts the Archive possessed. Clearly, Cliff Dodson had a deeper and more sinister reason for going after Aunt Elsie, and was hoping that no one would look beneath the surface for his true plot. Carrie, Chris knew, would say he was being paranoid.

Kevin McRae turned out to have been responsible for calling the police. "I recognized Dodson from when I did some work with the park service. There'd been threats," he explained. Dodson had apparently threatened park rangers for "hiding the gold for themselves," which meant that at the very least this guy was both vicious and significantly lacking in intelligence. Dr. McRae also admitted to having been suspicious of how Elsie had died. "And I'll admit part of it was simply self-interest," he explained. "What happened to Elsie

Kingsolver was a tragedy *and* just seemed too obviously an accident. I was worried that someone was after the Archive itself, and when my daughter mentioned being attacked on the road I decided it was imperative I call the police." But Chris doubted McRae was telling the whole story. *Why* did *you think Aunt Elsie's death was "too obviously an accident"?* Chris wondered. *And why come running over here as soon as you called the police—if that's really what you did?*

Chris and Carrie could add little, in the end, except that Dodson had broken through their picture window with a gun and gone right for them, a fact which Dodson thoroughly failed to explain. Chris and Carrie couldn't, either.

Or at least, Dodson failed to explain satisfactorily. He claimed, with much fidgeting and an even worse level of eye contact than before, to have assumed they had the gold because they were Aunt Elsie's relatives. When pressed, he could not explain why he assumed the kids would be carrying the gold, and tried to change his story by claiming that he wanted to search the house for the gold, and finally Detective Hermann irritably marched him out to a squad car and then shepherded the rest of the crowd out as well. Chris and Carrie did not mention the box they'd found in Aunt Elsie's office.

"Which may have been perjury," Carrie admitted worriedly much later, or earlier, in the morning. The police had left, McRae had announced he was going to go home and tell Maddison that everyone was fine and that the danger had passed, and Chris's parents, before going off to bed for a few hours, had declared that they were never leaving home again. Chris and Carrie had been left alone, so that Carrie could call her parents and attempt to explain what had happened. Instead they were trying to decide if they'd broken any laws by not mentioning the box.

"But everything Dodson and McRae said could have been true," Chris pointed out. "In which case, the box doesn't even enter into it."

"Uh huh," Carrie said, but she still looked unconvinced and worried. "And do you think the fact that my fingerprints are all over the gun will get me in trouble?" Chris told her he really didn't, partly because she'd admitted to that part of the story when the gun was bagged by a mildly impressed-looking deputy, and partly because the detective had looked thoroughly approving of her quick thinking. Although *Chris* still wasn't sure where Carrie had learned what to do with a gun . . .

"Mrs. Hadler did some interesting things before she became a secretary," Carrie said. Chris decided that if Carrie didn't want to tell him she didn't have to.

"Anyway," Chris said, "I'm the one who may have stolen evidence." And he dropped Carrie's locket into her lap.

"Oh my—*where* did you find this?" Carrie asked, gratifyingly astonished. "We looked everywhere!"

"Dodson must have gotten to it first," Chris said. "It was in that gym bag I grabbed from him. I snuck it into my pocket while everyone was staring at Mom and Dad."

"You snuck it out of the gym bag and into your

pocket that was then bagged as evidence," Carrie realized a moment later. "Chris!"

"I didn't realize what I was doing?"

"Our story will be that we found it under the couch after everyone had left," Carrie said decisively. She rubbed her thumb over the raised brass surface and then clasped the locket around her neck where it belonged. "If Dodson mentions it, we'll just admit that I *thought* I lost it in the office, but I must have been wrong because I found it under the couch this morning, several hours after the police had left. I was exhausted and not thinking straight at the time. Nobody suspects you of tampering with evidence at all, and the worst that happens is we have to give it up as evidence for a while."

"Then we'd better hope that they don't ask for it for a while," Chris said. "Because we may need it." Then he scrambled under his desk and unearthed the box, along with the notepad he'd been drawing on before Dodson so rudely interrupted, which he handed to

Carrie. Carrie tapped the rough sketch of the compass with one finger.

"The key was right in front of us the whole time?" she asked.

"The key was right in front of us the whole time," Chris agreed. "And," he realized, "Aunt Elsie split the clues between us."

"You don't think we missed a message on the locket itself?" Carrie asked. She'd reluctantly taken the locket off again, and was turning it over in her hands, looking for anything out of the ordinary. "Because I do not want to dunk the whole thing in lemon juice or roll it in ink or anything."

"If we need to we can try that later," Chris suggested. He set the box firmly on his desk. "But right now, I think we should try using it as a key." And he swung open the latch on the box.

It took some fumbling, and the chain on the locket got in the way at first, but then the slightly raised edges of the compass met the depressions in the keyhole, and with a faint click the locket settled in place. Chris took a deep breath, and, gingerly, with his eyes squeezed shut and his breath caught in his throat, turned the locket to the right, waiting with baited breath for—

"Uh, Chris?"

"Yeaaaaagh!" Chris yelped, and turned to stare at Carrie. She was staring right back at him, head tilted and eyebrows raised.

"What?" Chris demanded.

"Did you, by any chance," Carrie asked, fighting a grin, "watch *Indiana Jones* recently?"

"I don't see what that has to do with—"

"Because you're *bracing yourself* for a cursed whirlwind or ghosts or whatever you think is going to come bursting out of that box when it's opened," Carrie said. Chris deflated.

"Was I really?" he asked.

"You had your eyes closed and were leaning as far away from the box as humanly possible," Carrie said.

"Sorry," Chris said. "I got carried away. Do you want to do it?"

"No," Carrie said, and so firmly that Chris was

startled. "You started this, you decided to believe in it first, you should finish it," she said solemnly. "And besides," she added just as the lock clicked open and Chris lifted the lid of the box, "if the winds of the damned are going to come pouring out and fry the first person they see, better you than me."

"Seriously, Carrie?"

"Just saying." Carrie shrugged, and Chris lifted the lid all the way up with an irritated huff.

There was no cursed whirlwind, nor was there any unearthly light. There wasn't even a slight musty smell from old parchment or the gentle glow of precious metals, because there *were* no old fragments of parchment or gold and silver coins. There was instead a tightly folded packet of modern yellow legal paper wedged into the box, which when carefully unfolded proved to be nothing more than Aunt Elsie's notes on the exhibit on the 1717 Fleet. It was staggeringly disappointing. Chris handed the sheaf of papers to Carrie feeling dizzy with disappointment.

"Didn't you already find a copy of these in Aunt

Elsie's desk?" Carrie asked, leafing through the tightly creased pages.

"I did," Chris said. "And it looked exactly the same. I'm pretty sure I *saw her* write some of these that weekend in April I stayed at her house."

"Then why would she—wait," Carrie said, shaking a page free. "This isn't a note on the exhibit, it's another letter." She handed the rest of the papers to Chris, who began paging through them himself, only looking up when he realized Carrie was crying.

"Carrie?" he asked, startled.

"I need," Carrie said, stopped, started to put the letter down, decided halfway through the motion she should give it to Chris, and finally dropped it on the desk as if it were burning her, "I—need to call Mom and Dad, let them know what happened. And Maddison. I'll just—be in the living room."

She flicked the letter at Chris and darted out of the room, in the direction of the bathroom, which had the worst reception in the house. But Chris didn't think Carrie was thinking about phone reception. Carrie didn't look like she was going to go call anyone; actually, she looked like she was going to go break down sobbing where nobody could watch her, but maybe that was what she needed to do?

The letter, when Chris picked it up and smoothed it out as best as the creases would let him, was on the exact same yellow, lined legal pad paper as Aunt Elsie's notes, in blue ball point and flowing cursive. Aunt Elsie had written in a small hand so it was only one page front and back, and Chris ran a finger across the deep impressions her pen had cut before he picked out the address and started reading.

My dear Carrie and sweet, sweet Chris,

Smarty-pants, you figured it out. I never doubted for a second that you would, but I hope you didn't fight too much while you did. And I hate to say it to you, but such a big part of me wishes you didn't figure it out at all. This box and the things inside are not a gift. They are a terrible responsibility—a curse, if I'm honest—and one I pass on to you with deep misgivings. In fact, if I have died a natural death at the age of a hundred-and-three and Chris stumbles over this letter amongst my books, this need go no further. Burn the contents of this box, tell no one what you found, and rest assured that you have quietly closed the door on years of heartache.

But I very much fear that this is not the case, and so I tell you this. The notes on the 1717 Fleet exhibition you must have found in my office were incomplete. In the course of my ordinary research for the totally ordinary exhibit, I stumbled across references to a parish register from 1717 that contained an eyewitness account of the sinking of the San Telmo. *Chris, I suspect, has already tagged that ship as the holy grail of lost treasure ships. And Chris, sweetie, by this point you probably realize that I tried to shut you down when you asked me about the treasure. I can only say it was for a very good reason, and that at the time I genuinely thought the ship was lost to me forever. Since then, things have changed. I truly believe that with the information contained in my notes you can find the final resting place of the* San Telmo, *or at least put together enough information for a treasure hunter who you both trust to find it.*

But very few treasure hunters can be trusted, smaller Kingsolvers, and I fear that the reason you are reading this letter is because one who cannot has taken my life. Yes, I have my suspicions. In fact I think I know. No, I'm not going to tell you. I can't; if what I've pieced together over the last three weeks is true, the person who killed me would do anything to find this treasure, and even more to keep what they've done to get it a secret. I am not the first, nor will I likely be the last, to die. The one thing keeping you two safe is how little you suspect this person, and even then, I do not know how long that will protect you. The two of you are so very smart. You're probably going to figure out who it is from this letter alone.

So I am very sorry, but I can trust the two of you and only the two of you with this: take these notes and burn them, or take them and use them to find the San Telmo. *Either way, be very careful, be cautious in your trust, and remember, always and forever, that I love you.*

The notes Aunt Elsie had been talking about were on the third page of legal paper, part of a list of letters Aunt Elsie had been thinking of scanning and putting on the Archive website for the virtual exhibit. The clean copy of her notes, when Chris dug them out of the box in the garage where Aunt Helen had left them to be packed securely and stored in Aunt Elsie's house for the time being—a fact which had made Chris's dad moan about inheriting ghosts for a full half hour—just had a list of letters. One each from a Spanish survivor of the original wreck, an English privateer, a merchant who lost a vast amount of gold in the wreck, and a currently living local businessman who had found a piece of eight from the wreck while walking on the beach in the late eighties. But the notes Aunt Elsie had hidden included one more letter, from a deacon at Saint Erasmus's Church, dated 1735. The letter was supposed to describe the prayers the church offered for those killed in the 1717 disaster and the "melancholy" of the parish priest who witnessed the disaster, and next to the list Aunt Elsie had written, "Ship he witnessed? Possible eyewitness account?" Comparing the two almost identical sheets of paper, Chris realized she must have copied out a clean set of notes without reference to the deacon's letter and left them in her office.

Because Aunt Elsie had filled in the blanks. In a different shade of blue pen—which suggested that the research had taken her a while—she had amended the notes. Under "possible eyewitness account" she had scribbled "definite eyewitness account! Church documents from 1733 refer to event, *and* previous description of event!" And under "ship he witnessed?"

she had printed, and then almost scratched out in pen, "*San Telmo*."

Chris decided that his bedroom was too airless all of a sudden. The seriousness of the warning Aunt Elsie had included in her letter forced him to put the notes from the office in their proper place and close the box up before he practically fled into the back garden, where he had a small moment of hysterics among the hydrangeas.

Carrie found him collapsed on her favorite garden bench in the early morning sunlight, staring at the harmless little piece of yellow paper his aunt had died for.

"Nobody's ever found the *San Telmo*," Chris told her when she stuck her head out of his bedroom window and clambered down to sit next to him. "The amount of treasure they pulled from the *other* ships is insane, and there's a lot of uncertainty about which wreck is actually which, but as far as researchers know the *San Telmo* has never been found. Some say that's because it was faster and farther ahead when it went down."

"And some say it was cursed?" Carrie offered. Her eyes were puffy and her nose was red, but some of her prickliness had eased. Apparently crying her eyes out in the bathroom had been therapeutic.

"Not that I know of," Chris said. "Although, you know, this whole thing with Aunt Elsie might count."

Carrie groaned.

"Sorry, that was tasteless," Chris said. Carrie punched him in the shoulder.

"I have had," she said, "a terrible week. No, a terrible *month.* I've been *grieving,* Chris, and refusing to acknowledge it, and people have tried to kill us, and Mom and Dad are thinking of grounding me because apparently almost getting shot at is my fault, and to top it all off—has anyone told Professor Griffin what happened last night?"

"Oh *no.*"

"Do we even still have his keys?"

"Maybe?" Chris offered. He went through his

pockets while Carrie watched in horror, and luckily *did* find the professor's keys. That they were slightly stuck to a peppermint was survivable.

"I sort of want to kill you," Carrie said while clutching her hands in her hair in horror. "More than I usually do, I mean. My brain isn't making sense right now. And—oooh, I never called Maddison back either . . . she must be so confused, I know everything that's happened and I can't get *any* of it to make sense!"

"None of this makes a lot of sense," Chris pointed out, although he thought at least some of it did. He was now trying hard not to think about what conclusions Maddison might be drawing or what her father might be telling her. At the corner of the house a hummingbird investigated the feeder, and the dewdrops were fading off the grass. A beautiful early summer day was coming into its own, but Chris couldn't concentrate on it at all. Next to him, Carrie was distractedly shredding the grass at her feet, and he just sat and watched her for a while, trying to calm his mind, and remembering only too late that his mom was going to be horrified by the bald patch Carrie was digging.

"Things make more sense than they ever have before," Carrie pointed out finally, having organized her thoughts and run out of grass within easy reach. "We know why Aunt Elsie sent you that letter. We know why she left me the locket. We even helped put the person who killed her behind bars. We've done all she asked of us and more, Chris, and if you want to . . . " Carrie paused. "If you want to, we can stop right now."

"I know," Chris said. He folded the letter together with the notes and stuffed the resulting wad of papers in his pocket.

"But?" Carrie asked, and she did not sound surprised. Resigned and pained, yes, but not surprised.

"But I can't just leave it at this," Chris admitted. "Aunt Elsie asked us to either use these notes or destroy them, and I can't destroy her research. It mattered too much to her."

"I think that's why she asked us to burn the notes if

we couldn't, or wouldn't, find it," Carrie said. "*Because* it mattered so much to her."

"I know," Chris said. "But, well, why have you been going in and out through my bedroom window?"

Carrie hugged herself. "Because I can't settle," she said carefully. "Everything in the world is off-kilter. I keep thinking that the person we really need for this is, well, Aunt Elsie." Chris nodded. "And I know you're about to give me a terribly motivating speech," Carrie continued, "all about how it was her last request, etcetera, etcetera, ad nauseam, so I just want to check—you did catch the parts about danger and murder and heartbreak?"

"But it's for Aunt Elsie," Chris said. "And the discovery that should have been hers, and we can't just give up!"

"And what if we fail?" Carrie asked. "What if we don't give up, what if we go and try and we can't find the ship and all we do is lead whoever is out there killing people for this treasure right to it?"

"Then," Chris said, "we'll burn the notes and

salt the ashes and spread them over a swift-moving stream?"

Carrie froze in the middle of a retort to squint at him. "Did you borrow a book from Maddison?"

"Maybe," Chris admitted.

"That doesn't change my point," Carrie said.

"Or mine," Chris said stubbornly. He wasn't going to let this go. He didn't care how much he had to give up or, well, avoid, to solve this mystery, he *owed* it to Aunt Elsie.

"Danger, Chris," Carrie said. "Danger and murder and heartbreak, and Maddison is a total wildcard, and . . . "

"Aunt Elsie left us one last great puzzle," Chris said. "Can we really give up before we even *try* to solve it?"

"Most of her puzzles weren't likely to kill us," Carrie said. "And that was a terrible speech, and we need to go look up that priest who wrote the first-hand account." Chris opened his mouth to comment and she shushed him. "I'm not even going to pretend this is a good idea," Carrie said. "But I'll help."

"Yes! Help with what?"

"Aunt Elsie told us that a treasure map exists," Carrie said. "Now we need to find it."